ROY MORELLI

Steps Up to the Plate

Catch another great read by
THATCHER HELDRING!

Toby Wheeler: Eighth-Grade Benchwarmer

ROY MORELLI

MORELLI

Steps Up to the Plate

THATCHER HELDRING

A YEARLING BOOK

Text copyright © 2010 by Thatcher Heldring
Cover photograph copyright © by Jim Cummins/Corbis

All rights reserved. Published in the United States by Yearling, an imprint of Random House Children's Books, a division of Random House, Inc., New York. Originally published in hardcover in the United States by Delacorte Press, an imprint of Random House Children's Books, New York, in 2010.

Yearling and the jumping horse design are registered trademarks of Random House, Inc.

Visit us on the Web! www.randomhouse.com/kids
Educators and librarians, for a variety of teaching tools, visit us at www.randomhouse.com/teachers

The Library of Congress has cataloged the hardcover edition of this work as follows:
Heldring, Thatcher.
Roy Morelli steps up to the plate / Thatcher Heldring. — 1st ed.
p. cm.
Summary: When eighth-grader Roy Morelli's divorced parents find out he is failing history, they ban him from playing on his beloved all-star baseball team, and, even worse, he winds up being tutored by his father's new girlfriend.
ISBN 978-0-385-73391-5 (trade) — ISBN 978-0-385-90406-3 (lib. bdg.) — ISBN 978-0-375-89343-8 (ebook)
[1. Baseball—Fiction. 2. Schools—Fiction. 3. Divorce—Fiction. 4. Conduct of life—Fiction.]
I. Title. II. Title: Roy Morelli Steps Up to the Plate.
PZ7.H3734 Ro 2010   [Fic]—dc22   2009033845

ISBN 978-0-440-23978-9 (pbk.)

Printed in the United States of America
10 9 8 7 6 5 4 3 2 1

First Yearling Edition 2011

To my history teachers,
who introduced me to some real characters

· 1 ·

"Three more," Dad said, stepping off the mound.

"Make 'em count," I told him, wiggling the bat.

We were on one of the eight ball fields that surrounded the grandstand, the small, half-covered stadium that sat in the middle of Boardman Park. Baseball season started next week, and I needed to shake off the winter rust.

"What do you want?" Dad called. He was tall, like me, but heavy. He was wearing jeans and a faded green Pilchuck High School T-shirt. His hair hung over the top of his ears, like it had for as long as I could remember.

"Whatever you got, old-timer," I said, twisting my toe into the dirt, imagining this was the last inning of the biggest game of my life.

"Old-timer?" Dad asked, like he hadn't heard me right.

"That's what I said." I tugged on my ear and pointed to Dad. "Maybe you should adjust that hearing aid."

Dad gripped all three baseballs in his right hand and held them out for me to see. "You know what these are?" he asked.

"What?"

"Strike one, strike two, and strike three."

I shook my head and smiled. "No way, old man."

He stepped back onto the mound. "First pitch," he said, bending forward to start his windup.

"Just make sure it comes with mustard."

Dad smiled. "Order up." He leaned back, then stepped into a breaking ball that curved to the outside corner as it crossed the plate.

I saw the movement on the ball, but swung too late to catch up.

Strike one.

I slid my hands back down the barrel and pointed at Dad. "Another one," I said.

Dad nodded.

Same pitch. This time, I swung earlier but got underneath it, fouling it behind me.

Strike two.

"Time," I said, backing away from the plate. I took two practice cuts.

On the mound, Dad wiped his hands on his jeans,

then went to work. He planted his left foot, lifted his right leg, and with an extra kick, whipped his third pitch toward me.

Wait for it, I told myself, expecting the ball to break away again. But the ball never broke. It barreled straight down the middle of the strike zone. By the time I saw my mistake, it was too late. I took a hack, but the ball chugged past me. It slammed against the top plank of the backstop, then ricocheted halfway back to the plate.

Strike three.

Down on three pitches. Ouch. I stood at the plate, staring at my shoes. I would have to do better than that when baseball season started. I was on the Pilchuck All-Star team, and I knew from last season that the pitchers threw some serious smoke. It was nothing like the rec league games I had seen my friends Kenny and Fish play in, where the pitches came in nice and easy. I had to be ready. Just yesterday Coach Burke had told me he expected big things from me this season.

Holding the bat in one hand, I picked up the ball and tossed it to Dad.

"Not bad for an old-timer, huh?" he said.

"The sun was in my eyes," I joked as we began gathering up the rest of the baseballs scattered around the infield.

"Face it, Roy," Dad said, patting his stomach. "Your old man's still got it."

"You mean *that*?" I asked, pointing to his gut.

Dad rubbed his belly. "This?" he asked proudly, pointing to himself. "This is all muscle."

"I didn't know fat was a muscle," I said.

"It was enough to strike *you* out," Dad said as he put his arm around me. "And believe me, that's not easy."

"Well, don't let it go to your head," I said.

Dad dropped a dozen baseballs into a canvas bag. "I'm serious, Roy. I know how talented you are and how hard you work. I'm proud of you."

Just then, I heard the sound of a car door opening in the small parking lot beside the field. Quickly, I spotted Mom plowing toward us like a one-woman army.

"Incoming," I said to Dad, who had his back to her.

Dad looked up, then muttered something under his breath. "What time is it?" he asked.

"Time for you to say a prayer," I told him.

Mom and Dad had been divorced for five years, but they both still lived in Pilchuck. That meant my sixteen-year-old sister, Sara, and I lived by *the schedule*. Every other weekend with Dad, the rest of the time with Mom.

That afternoon, I was supposed to be home by five o'clock for dinner and homework—even though it was Friday. It was sundown now, which meant it was at least seven-thirty.

Oops.

Giving me the *stay* hand, Dad jogged over to meet

Mom. "We're just wrapping it up," he said. "I guess we lost track of time."

"Lost track of time?" Mom repeated. "Mike, you sound like one of the kids."

Mom and Dad were standing face to face on the first baseline like an ump and a manager going nose to nose over a close call. I was hovering near the pitcher's mound.

"Tee," he said. "Relax."

Mom's name was Teresa. I knew she didn't like Dad's nickname for her, but I had heard her call him worse. Things had never gotten super ugly between them, but there had definitely been a lot of shouting.

"We had a deal, Mike. Roy was supposed to be at home an hour and a half ago. He has homework to do."

"It's Friday," said Dad. "He has all weekend."

"Yes, but you and I both know he'll be out here playing baseball all weekend. Then it's Sunday night and nothing's gotten done."

Dad held up his hands. "Okay," he said, waving the white flag, "he's all yours." Then he turned to me and whistled, like I hadn't been able to hear every word of their conversation. "Let's call it a day," he said.

Knowing I had no choice, I made my way over to Mom.

"Hi, sweetie," she said, reaching up to me. Unlike my brown hair, her hair was blond and down to her shoulders.

"I'll be in the car," she told us.

"We'll pick this up later," Dad said after Mom walked away.

"Tomorrow?"

Dad shook his head. "Next week."

"What's wrong with tomorrow?"

"I have a . . . an appointment."

"You mean a date."

Dad was quiet for a second. "You're right," he admitted after a moment. "I mean a date."

"With the teacher?" I asked.

"With Camille," said Dad, nodding.

As far as I could tell, Camille had been in the picture for about a month. But Dad was already talking about introducing her to me and Sara.

"If it was me, I'd rather play baseball," I said.

"Next week, Roy. I promise."

I wondered why he couldn't make the date wait instead of me, but I couldn't find the right way to say it. Dad and I were pros at joking around but not so good at talking about feelings. "Make sure you wear a big shirt so your muscles don't hang out."

Dad laughed and gave me a quick hug. We left it with a fist bump. Then I turned and walked across the grass to the car, where Mom was waiting.

Later that evening, I wandered into the kitchen for a soda. Mom and Sara were sitting at the white table where the three of us ate dinner whenever we were all home at the same time, which wasn't very often.

During the day, Mom went to her job at an insurance company, which she said was "okay for now." Three nights a week, she went to the community college, where she was taking business classes. Why anyone would *choose* to go to school was a huge mystery to me. That evening, she was marking up a textbook with a pink highlighter.

"Something came for you," said Sara, barely looking up from her phone. She was busy texting. Probably Izzy, one of her friends. Sara had darker hair than either me or Mom, which she wore in bangs over her forehead.

"Where?" I asked, wondering what it could be. I didn't get mail very often.

"On the refrigerator."

I scanned the refrigerator door. There were pictures of me and Sara. Notes from Mom to herself about places she had to be and stuff she had to do. I saw a biology test with Sara's name on it and an A+ circled in blue ink. Sara claimed it was embarrassing that Mom still put her tests and papers on the refrigerator. I knew it was an act, though. If it was *really* embarrassing, she would have taken it down.

Finally, I spotted a brochure with the words *Orientation Packet* printed on the cover. It was from Pilchuck High School, where I'd be going next year.

I glanced at the brochure, then reached into the fridge for a soda. "I'll be in my room," I said after cracking open the can. I left the brochure where I found it.

"Take the packet with you," Mom said. "It has some information about the classes you need to take."

"Sounds fascinating."

"Take it, Roy. And don't forget, you have a chapter of history to read."

"Tonight? It's Friday."

"Before you watch television or play any baseball this weekend, you're going to read for at least an hour."

I was about to protest when Sara jumped up, grabbed her coat, and made a beeline for the door. "Later," Sara said. "I'm going to Izzy's."

"Be home by ten," Mom said.

"Why doesn't she have to read?" I asked.

Sara pointed to the refrigerator. "Do you see that A-plus?" she asked. "That's why." Then she flew out the front door and down the steps.

"You really expect me to do homework on a Friday?" I said, pleading with Mom.

"Just one hour, Roy."

"Fine," I said, snatching the brochure from the refrigerator. "But if I die of boredom, don't let Sara have any of my stuff."

I sat at my desk, opened my history book, and flipped to the chapter that my history teacher, Mr. Downer, had assigned. But then I saw the title of the chapter: "Andrew Jackson and the Nullification Crisis." Big snore. My brain shut down and I closed the book. It didn't matter; we'd be reading the same chapter out loud on Monday.

I checked my clock. I had fifty-eight and a half minutes to kill. So I picked up the brochure. I wasn't expecting much, but to my surprise, the more I read, the more I liked.

The brochure said there were nine hundred sixty-seven students at Pilchuck High School. *What a crowd!* I thought, leaning back in my chair. I could see it now. I'd be the baseball king. By day, I'd rule the hallways with my teammates. The girls would follow me in a pack, led by none other than Valerie Hopkins, the finest of them all. By night, I'd play under the lights in front of a thousand people. And wherever I went, everyone in the school would see me and say, *That's Roy Morelli. Have you seen him play yet?*

Who needed history when I had a future like *that*?

• 2 •

"Look," said Derek on Sunday afternoon. "Coach Harden's here."

We were standing on the field in the Boardman Park grandstand. We had come for a preseason, players-only workout. I looked into the nearly empty wooden bleachers and spotted Coach Harden easily. He was sitting ten or eleven rows up from the first-base dugout. Coach Burke was there too, wearing a blue All-Star hat. But it was Coach Harden we were most excited to see.

"I heard he was coming," said Ruben, who was stretching nearby. "I didn't believe it, though. I wonder how long he's been there."

Derek shrugged. "I'm surprised he's here at all. I

figured he'd be too busy with his own team to watch us take batting practice."

Bull Harden was the varsity baseball coach at Pilchuck High School, and the only person from Pilchuck ever to play major league baseball—so far.

"Coach Harden's not here to coach," I said. "He's here to scout."

"Scout?" Derek asked. "Scout who?"

"Us," I said, picking up a bat and taking a slow practice swing. "He's here to check out the talent."

In Pilchuck, high school baseball was like the major leagues, and the All-Star team was like Triple-A. We were one step away from the big show. And by next spring, that was where I expected to be—in the big show, playing shortstop for Coach Harden.

"If he's looking for talent, he better keep his eyes on the Mooch."

I looked over and rolled my eyes at Moochie Goodman. "I hope he brought binoculars," I said.

"What's that supposed to mean?" Moochie asked, sliding a beat-up batting helmet over his dark, curly hair.

Ruben held his hand waist-high. "It means you put the short back in shortstop, Montgomery."

Moochie grabbed a bat. "That's funny, because shortstop is where I'm going to be playing next spring, Morelli," he said.

"Don't make me laugh," I said, clutching my sides. "You're not even the starting shortstop on *this* team."

"Yeah," said Derek. "And I got a million dollars that says you won't be the one playing shortstop on the high school team either."

Moochie adjusted his helmet, then tapped the plate with his bat. "You're laughing now, but you'll be crying later," he told me.

I watched Moochie take his first four or five swings. I hadn't seen him play since last spring. Back then, he swung at everything. Now, he was keeping his weight back, being patient, really turning on pitches. *Good*, I thought. *When I beat him out for shortstop next spring, it will mean even more.*

"You really think Coach Harden's here to see us?" asked Derek.

I turned away from Moochie. "He has seven seniors to replace next year," I explained. "He knows we're going to be ninth graders in the fall. He came to see the future."

"So the All-Star team is like his farm system?" said Derek.

Ruben nodded. "And we're the prospects."

I'm one of Bull Harden's prospects, I thought. I liked the sound of that. I looked into the stands again and waited for my turn at bat. Just knowing Coach Harden was watching made me want to knock the cover off the ball.

Moochie blasted a drive to right field. He stood next to home plate, watching the ball until it landed a few feet from the wall. He puffed his chest out so far I thought I could pop it with a pin. "That's what the Mooch brought," he said, tossing me the bat.

"Look out, Roy," said Derek. "The Mooch is making his move. Are you worried?"

Worried? Please. I stepped to the plate like I owned it.

In the outfield, one of the fielders moved toward Moochie's ball. "Leave it!" I shouted, shaking my head. Then, before I dug in, I gave Coach Harden a wave. Not a big dorky wave. Just a quick wave so *he* knew *I* knew he was there.

Lights, camera, action. It was showtime. Better yet, Roytime.

I was going to end this business with Moochie *right now*. The Mooch had to know he was playing in Roy's world.

The first pitch came. I swung late and shanked a foul ball over the backstop.

On the next pitch, I swung earlier. *Plink.* Right center.

Next pitch. *Plink.* Center.

After a couple more cuts, I got into a rhythm. The foul balls turned into hard-hit grounders. And the grounders turned into line drives. After a while, line drives were deep drives into the gap.

"Hey, Morelli," Derek called from the on-deck circle. "I thought it was ten swings. You're way over."

"Couple more," I said, without looking away. I was in the zone, and I didn't want to stop.

Moochie's ball was the target. And I went for it, again and again. I didn't hold anything back. I just kept dropping baseballs in right field until the grass had turned white.

When the pitcher ran out of baseballs, I let go of the bat and shook my hands out. My fingers had been locked in a clench, and my palms were starting to burn.

"One more," I said to the pitcher.

The pitch was a fastball, waist-high over the plate. A beauty. I opened my stance, shifted my weight back, and whipped the bat forward through the strike zone, clubbing the ball on the sweet spot, sending it into deep right field.

It cleared the wall by a foot.

Put that in the history books, I thought, flipping the bat toward the ground, barrel-first. It bounced once, then jumped back into my hands like it was on a string.

I handed the bat off to Derek, grabbed my glove, and hustled out to the field to help shag balls. Along the way, I took one last look at Coach Harden. This time, I swore he nodded.

· 3 ·

On Monday, I sat in the back of Mr. Downer's history class with my friends Kenny and Fish. Fish's real name was Nathan Fishman, but nobody called him that. We became friends in fourth grade, when we got roles together in the holiday pageant—and got kicked out of the play on the first day of rehearsal for having sword fights with our walking sticks.

After that, we played baseball together in elementary school. We stayed tight, even when I moved on to the All-Star team in sixth grade and they stayed in the Pilchuck rec league.

I yawned as Wyatt began reading out loud from his textbook. Wyatt was one of the smallest guys in the eighth grade. His voice was so soft everyone called him Quiet Wyatt.

"Speak up, Wyatt," said Mr. Downer. In exactly two minutes, he would point his bony finger at someone else while the rest of us followed along.

Fish, Kenny, and I had our books open, but we weren't paying attention to Wyatt. We were playing a game called bagball. It was pretty easy, especially with a teacher like Mr. Downer, who slept like an old dog. We crumpled up a piece of paper until it was the size of a marble, then tried to toss it into someone's bag. We played it like H-O-R-S-E, so if one of us made a shot and someone else missed, whoever missed got a letter.

It might have been a big waste of time, but so was history.

"You're up," Kenny said to Fish after landing a bagball into a red backpack a few rows up.

Fish pinched a wad of paper between his thumb and pointer finger. "Locked and loaded," he said, aiming for the red backpack. With a flick of the wrist, the wad was airborne. It had a nice arc, but it drifted right, landing on the floor next to the desk. "Man," Fish said. "The breeze caught it."

"That's *H-O-R*," I told him, rubbing it in.

"Let's see you do better," said Fish.

Across the room, Mr. Downer pointed his finger at Megan, who began reading something about pioneers. It was the same stuff they'd been ramming down our throats since fourth grade.

For now, I needed a target. It didn't take me long to

find one. Two rows up and one row over was a big brown shoulder bag hanging off the corner of a chair. The bag belonged to Valerie. Her old boyfriend, JJ, had moved to California last month, so she was on her own again. Now was my chance to get her attention.

"Valerie's bag," I said, picking my target.

"Are you sure?" Kenny asked. "She's not gonna be happy about you throwing paper at her bag."

"She's going to *act* like she's not happy," I explained. "But deep down, she'll love it."

"Roy's right," said Fish. "Why do you think she's on the social committee? Because she gets to make all those announcements over the PA and be onstage during assemblies. She loves attention."

"It's just my way of saying hello," I told them as I lined up my shot. Valerie's light blond hair was cupped in her hand. I got ready to fire. Suddenly, Valerie shifted in her seat and the flap of the bag fell closed, blocking the hoop.

"What now?" Kenny asked.

"Automatic letter," said Fish.

"No way," I said back. "She moved."

"Those are the rules of bagball. Sorry."

"I'm not going down like that," I said, watching Mr. Downer's eyes grow heavy. Staying in a crouch, I made my way up the aisle to Valerie's desk. All I had to do was nudge her bag to the left and we'd have a hoop again. I slipped my finger beneath the strap and slid it sideways. I turned back to see if it was far enough.

"A little more," Kenny mouthed, gesturing to the left.

I moved it a little more and looked back again.

"Too far," said Fish, waving his hand the other way.

I reached up one last time. But I reached too far, and my hand ended up inside the bag. Something rattled. Valerie looked down and saw me.

"Hey! What are you doing?" she asked, jerking the bag toward her. Then she saw the wad of paper in my hand. "Are you putting *spitballs* in my bag?"

"It's just paper," I whispered to Valerie. "No spit. You have nothing to worry about. You look nice today."

Then I hustled back to my seat.

"What happened?" Fish asked.

"She thinks they're spitballs," I said.

"Did you tell her they're just paper?"

"She wouldn't listen."

"Women," said Fish. "They're unreasonable."

Suddenly, Mr. Downer was looking right at me. "Mr. Morelli," he said, "would you like to join our conversation, or should we join yours?"

"What are we talking about?" I asked, sitting up straight.

"We were discussing the role of women in society."

Fish grinned. "That's what we were talking about too, Mr. Downer."

"I'm *so* sorry to interrupt," said Mr. Downer sarcastically.

"That's okay," I said. "We were finished anyway."

Fish and I exchanged a look as everyone in the class laughed. "Nice save," I said.

"I got your back," he said with a smile.

"Your *way* back," we both said before cracking up.

Mr. Downer snapped his fingers and we went back to reading from the textbook. Ten long minutes later, the bell rang. Everyone got busy stuffing books and paper into their bags. I was heading to the door when Mr. Downer stopped me. "I'd like a word with you, please."

"This won't take long," I told Fish and Kenny. "I'll catch up with you in a minute."

When they were gone, I walked up to Mr. Downer's cluttered desk. "You wanted to see me?" I said.

"Yes, I did," said Mr. Downer, scratching the tip of his nose. A snowfall of skin flakes floated onto his grade book. "I'll get right to the point. Your performance in this class is unsatisfactory."

I had a feeling Mr. Downer had a different definition of satisfactory than I did. All I wanted to do was get through the school year and move on to high school.

"I thought I did pretty good on the last test," I said.

"You got a thirty-seven," Mr. Downer replied. "Out of a hundred. Let me explain this in a way you'll understand. On the baseball field, a .370 batting average might be something to brag about. But in here, .370 is unacceptable."

Typical, I thought as Mr. Downer kept talking. It was like I was some foreign exchange student who only spoke baseball. How dumb did he think I was?

". . . Now, in order to pass the class, you must average a B on the next test and the final exam." Mr. Downer rubbed his temples. "Class participation will also count, but I suggest you focus on the exams."

"I'm sorry, Mr. Downer. I'll try harder. I promise," I said, just wanting to get out of there. I had better things to do with my life than listen to some fossil lecture me about my future.

"I'll believe it when I see it," he said. Then he pointed to the door. "You're dismissed, Mr. Morelli."

What a load, I thought, leaving the room. Mr. Downer was blaming me for bombing a test, when he was the one who never taught us anything! It was totally unfair. Why should I waste my time memorizing the names of all those dead people just so I could get a good grade on some test—especially since Mr. Downer didn't seem to care about history either?

On the way home from school that day, I stopped at Dad's apartment. It was only a few minutes out of the way, and I wanted to tell him about Coach Harden and see if he'd pitch to me again, like he'd promised.

I knew he was home because his truck was parked out front. Dad was a general contractor, which meant he remodeled houses and sometimes built new ones from scratch. He used to work for a bigger company, but a few months ago, he started his own business, Morelli Construction.

Dad was in the kitchen, spraying the sink and wiping it down with a rag.

"You'll never believe who I saw yesterday," I said, dropping my bag on the floor. "Coach Harden. He was scouting. And, Dad, I was on fire."

"Good for you, Roy. You caught Coach Harden's eye. That's a big deal." Dad inspected the counter for a minute, then opened an empty drawer with a shrug and tossed in the rag. "Good enough," he said to himself. Then he turned back to me. "Sounds like you're on your way."

"I wish I was in high school *now*," I said, falling back into a big brown chair that faced the kitchen from the living room. I picked at the duct tape that ran across the arm like a racing stripe and spun myself in slow circles.

Dad went to the sink and rinsed a glass, then put it on the drying rack. "You're almost there," he said. "Just two more months until summer."

I noticed a thick paperback book lying on the coffee table. *"A People's History of the United States,"* I said. "Is this yours, Dad?"

"I borrowed it," he said.

I dropped the book and it fell to the table with a thud. "For what? To kill ants?"

"To read," he said.

I almost laughed. "I've never seen you read a book."

Dad leaned forward over the counter. "Well, I'm reading one now."

"But why *this*?"

"I told Camille I wanted to know more about history and she suggested it."

"Man, I would never read a book just because a girl suggested it. You must really like her."

Dad smiled like a fool in love. "I do really like her. She's great. She makes me happy."

She made him happy? What was I—dog meat?

He pushed himself back from the counter. "Anyway, I'm really into this. I'm learning a lot about history. It makes me wish I'd paid more attention in school."

Ugh. Not *him* too.

I watched him open the refrigerator and begin pushing jars and cartons around. Then he stood up straight, snapped his fingers, and closed the door. "I can't believe I forgot salad dressing," he said. "You want to come to the grocery store with me? I'll drop you off at your mom's on the way home."

"Can we stop by the ball fields?" I asked. "I brought my glove."

Dad shook his head. "I wish I could, pal," he said,

grabbing his wallet. "But Camille's coming over for dinner."

"Again? You just saw her Friday. Can we at least hit tomorrow?"

"You got it," he said, scooping up his keys. "Coming?"

I threw my backpack over my shoulder and followed Dad out of the apartment. "That's okay. I think I'll walk," I said.

Back at home, I opened my history book and tried to read a chapter about taxes in the colonies. I flipped through the pages, hoping for maps, but it was all dates and names. It was too much. I would get to the end of a sentence and not even remember what the sentence was about. How could I remember a whole *chapter*? That was the problem with history. It was all about memorizing, and I wasn't a good memorizer. Why didn't Mr. Downer get that?

As I pushed my history book away, I could hear Sara on the phone in the living room.

"Iz," she was saying. "I'm telling you how to do it. You have to subtract two from the other side of the equation to get X. . . . Hold on . . . I love this commercial. . . . Yes, Iz, that's the quadratic formula. What do you mean, the what?"

I shook my head as I listened to Sara. It was amazing how she could study, talk on the phone, and watch

TV at the same time. I couldn't even read for two minutes without getting lost. Giving up on history for the
night, I picked up my earth sciences book instead and
opened to a chapter on the water cycle. It had to be
better than reading about taxes in the colonies.

· 4 ·

The next afternoon, Fish, Kenny, and I were sitting at my kitchen table, rubbing shaving cream into our gloves, when we heard footsteps outside.

"That's my mom," I said. "Don't say anything about the history test."

"She doesn't know?" Kenny asked.

"No," I said. "I haven't gotten around to telling her yet."

A second later, the door opened.

"Hey, Mom," I said.

"Hi, boys," Mom answered. She set her purse on the counter and unbuttoned her coat.

"Hi, Mrs. Morelli," said Kenny.

"How was school today?" she asked.

"I got a B on my math test," I said. Unlike history,

math made sense to me. It was easy to see why it was a class in school. Who didn't want to know how to count?

"Good for you," said Mom. "How about your other classes? Did you get that history test back yet?"

"Um, nope. Not yet."

"How do you think you did?" Mom asked.

"About the same," I said.

"About the same as what?" Mom asked.

"Um . . ."

"About the same as us," said Fish. "We all studied together, so we'll probably get the same grades. When we get the test back."

"Which hasn't happened yet," Kenny added.

Technically, that wasn't a lie. Mr. Downer had only *told* me about my grade yesterday. He hadn't actually passed the tests back. He wouldn't do that until later this week.

I wasn't sure if Mom believed us. But before she could ask any more questions, Sara wandered in from the living room. "What's with the shaving cream?" she asked us.

"It softens the leather," I explained.

Sara shrugged. "Well, at least you can use it for something."

I stuck my foot out to trip Sara as she passed by, but she stepped right over it. She walked to the other side of the kitchen and slumped against the refrigerator.

"How's my girl?" Mom asked.

Sara blew her bangs off her forehead. "Okay."

"Just okay?"

"Mr. Clawson didn't like my essay on *The Grapes of Wrath.*"

What was this? Did the honor-roll student finally bite the big one at school? I was on the edge of my seat, waiting for the good news.

"What do you mean, he didn't like it?" Mom asked. "Did he tell you that?"

"No," Sara replied. "He gave me a B. It's totally unfair."

Mom squeezed Sara's hand. "Sweetie, you can't get an A on everything." Then she said to both of us, "I'm going to take a quick nap before class. There's lasagna in the fridge for dinner. I'll be home by eight o'clock." She looked at me. "Roy, please do your homework before you meet your dad." She looked Sara in the eye. "There's nothing wrong with a B," she said before going to her room.

"I worked hard on that essay," Sara called after her.

"Not hard enough," I said.

Sara scowled at me. "Oh, you should talk. When's the last time you got an A in anything besides gym?"

"I got an A in Spanish," said Fish.

"Bueno," Sara said, then went back to the living room.

A few minutes later, we had put our gloves away.

Fish and Kenny were getting ready to go. "You have time to swing by Pilchuck Market?" Fish asked.

"I can't," I said. "But let's go Friday. Right after school."

"Yeah," said Kenny, elbowing Fish. "You never know who might be there."

"Maybe somebody whose name rhymes with Smalarie," Fish teased as the door closed in his face.

I went back into the kitchen. I was only alone for a minute before Sara reappeared. "Did I hear you say you're meeting Dad?" she asked.

"Yeah. At the park. Why?"

Sara pulled a soda out of the refrigerator. "Because Dad took Camille to the art museum in Seattle."

"Who told you that?"

"Dad."

"You're crazy," I said, going to the door.

Sara shrugged. "I'm just telling you what he told me earlier. If you want to interrupt his date, be my guest."

I hopped on my bike and rolled west down Verlot Street. I crossed Boardman Street, with the high school on one side and the middle school on the other, and made my way through downtown Pilchuck. I cruised past Pete's Sporting Goods, with the clearance-sale banner for skis and snowboards, then cut through the parking lot of the new Landover Lumber store.

When I got to Dad's building, I locked up my bike, then took the steps two at a time to his apartment.

With a quick knock, I slipped my key in the door and went inside.

The kitchen was empty. "Dad," I called. "Are you here?"

I took another step in.

That was when I heard someone—definitely not Dad—say, "Hello?"

A moment later, I was looking at a woman with light red curly hair and green eyes. She was fair-skinned, had freckles on her nose, and was wearing gray slacks with a white shirt under a dark sweater. I noticed there were chalk marks on her pants.

"Hello," said the woman, studying me. "I'm Camille. And you must be Roy?"

"Yeah," I said. "Is my dad here?"

"He's in the other room," Camille told me. Then she turned toward the hallway. "Mike?" she called.

"Be right there," I heard Dad reply.

Camille and I stood there in silence. In the kitchen, the faucet dripped. Upstairs, one of Dad's neighbors slammed a door shut. The blinds rattled in the breeze.

"So, um, you're a teacher?" I asked.

"That's right," said Camille. "At the high school. And you're in eighth grade?"

"Yup."

"So you'll be at the high school next year."

Oh, good, I thought. *Maybe we can meet in the cafeteria and have more thrilling conversations like this one.*

Finally, Dad bounded into the living room. But instead of his normal work clothes—cargo pants, sweatshirt, and his old green hat—he was dressed in nice pants and a button-down shirt. "All set?" he asked, fiddling with the button on the end of his sleeve.

When there was no answer, he looked up. That was when he saw me. "Hey, pal," he said, sounding surprised. "What's up?"

"Are we playing ball?" I asked Dad. By then, the answer was obvious, but I wanted to hear him say it.

Dad rubbed his chin like he did when he was nervous. "I'm real sorry, Roy. I blew it. There's an exhibit at the art museum. These tickets fell into my lap and . . ."

"The art museum?" I asked. "Really?"

Camille turned to Dad. "Mike, we can do this some other time. If you had plans—"

"No, no," he told her in an upbeat voice. "The tickets are for today."

"Well, um . . ." Camille hesitated. "Okay, I guess I'll be in the car." She offered her hand to me. "Roy, it was very nice to meet you."

"You too," I said as she left the apartment. *Not.*

When Dad and I were alone, he said, "I promise, pal. We'll hit the park this weekend."

"My first practice is this weekend. I'm gonna be kind of busy."

Dad should have told me we would find a way. But he didn't say that. Instead, he looked over at the front door, then back at me, and said, "Maybe this is a good time to do some homework, huh?"

"Uh, yeah, sure, homework," I said, wondering whose idea *that* was.

"How about a ride home?" Dad asked.

I told him I had my bike. He gave me a pat on the shoulder, then hustled after Camille, leaving me alone in the living room. Through the window, I could see him jump in the truck, then lean over. My view of the passenger side was blocked, but I had seen enough.

• 5 •

By Friday afternoon, I had made up my mind to give Dad another chance. It was my weekend with him, and I didn't want to spoil it by holding a grudge. Plus, I was in a better mood anyway. Our first real practice of the season was just one day away, and I couldn't wait to take the field.

Right before history class that day, I ran into Ruben and Derek in the hallway. "Just the guy we were looking for," said Ruben.

"What's up?" I asked.

"We're headed to Boardman Park after school," said Derek. "The whole team's gonna be there."

"You're just telling me now?" I asked.

"We only started talking about it at lunch," Ruben answered, "but we couldn't find you."

"I was shooting hoops out back," I said.

"Are you in?" Derek asked.

"Yeah," I said as I walked away. "Definitely. I'll see you there."

I had only gone a few steps when Fish appeared next to me. "You'll see them where?" he asked.

"Boardman Park," I said. "For batting practice."

"Today?" Fish asked.

"Yeah, after school."

"Aren't you forgetting something?" he asked.

"What?"

"You said you were coming to Pilchuck Market."

Fish was right. I'd forgotten all about that. But I couldn't skip batting practice. Not the day before the season started. "I'm sorry, man. We'll have to do it some other time."

"Hey, it's your life," Fish said as we cruised down the hallway. Up ahead, Valerie was standing in a circle with the rest of the Social Committee. She gave me the evil eye as we passed them. Still, at least she looked at me.

"I hope Coach Harden will be there," I said.

"I thought he coached the high school team."

"He likes to scout," I said. "It's kind of a big deal. You know he played thirty-six games for the Cubs before he got hurt? He's practically a legend."

"I know, I know," said Fish. "He hit eight homers and threw out nine base runners. It doesn't make him a legend."

"Most guys don't even make it to the big leagues," I said. "But Coach Harden did. That makes him a legend around here."

"Fine," said Fish. "He's a legend. You and your All-Star buddies can carve a statue of him."

Why does Fish have to rain on my parade? I wondered as we approached Kenny. *Can't he see how important this is to me?*

"Who's a legend?" Kenny asked. He was waiting for us by the bathrooms, wearing unlaced sneakers with no socks and long shorts that covered his knees.

"Coach Harden," I said. Kenny and I were side by side now. Fish was hanging back.

"I heard they might name the grandstand after him," Kenny said.

"Why?" said Fish from behind. "Because he played twenty-six games with the Cubs?"

"*Thirty*-six," I said, turning around. "He's also won two state championships at Pilchuck High School."

"Yeah, like twenty years ago," said Fish.

"Ten," Kenny corrected him.

"Great," said Fish as we made our way into the classroom. "That's fascinating."

Fish's sarcasm could get on my nerves sometimes. "What do you have against Coach Harden?" I asked him.

"Nothing," he replied as class began. "Forget it. Let's just play bagball."

We opened our books with everyone else, then

picked up where we had left off the last time we played—the same day Mr. Downer had lectured me about my grades. After that, we'd decided to take a break until the dust settled.

A few rows over, McKlusky was reading about the war with Mexico. Mr. Downer was slouched at his desk, picking specks of wax out of his ears. If the power went out, we could make candles to last a week with the wax he had mined just in the last scoop.

"What do you have?" I asked Kenny.

"*H-O,*" he said, crumpling up a piece of paper.

"Fish?"

"*H-O-R.*"

"*H* for me, chumps," I said.

I heard McKlusky tripping over a word. "Sec . . . Sess . . . Secsess . . ." McKlusky and I had played on the basketball team together. Good thing he had never stumbled on the court like he was stumbling in class.

"Secession," Mr. Downer said sleepily.

"Secession," McKlusky repeated, and kept going.

Fish leaned over. "*H,* for now," he said. "You still have to make it into Valerie's bag."

"I could do it with my eyes closed."

Fish looked at me skeptically. "Prove it."

That did it. Once Fish told me to prove it, I had to do it.

"And you can't just close your eyes," said Kenny. "You have to be blindfolded."

I looked around the room. Mr. Downer's head was bobbing. Cassandra had just started reading. I had at least two minutes. "You still got that blue bag you brought your lunch in?" I asked Fish.

Fish handed me a large blue canvas bag. With one last glance at Downer, I slipped the bag over my head.

"Can you see?" asked Kenny.

"No."

"How many fingers am I holding up?" asked Fish.

"What's that gonna prove?" Kenny asked. "He'd just lie."

"I can't see," I said. "Just hand me some paper."

To make the shot, I had to concentrate. I knew about where Valerie's desk was. From there, I just needed the right touch. Feeling the bagball in my fingers, I pulled my hand back and lofted a shot in the right direction.

I didn't need my eyes to know where it landed.

"Oh, gross!" Valerie shouted before I had the bag off my head. By the time I could see again, everyone was staring at me, including Mr. Downer. Valerie was up out of her seat, marching toward me. "I told you to keep your spit wads away from my desk!" she said.

"They're not spit wads," said Fish.

"It's just bagball," Kenny added, as if Valerie should know.

"I don't care what they are. They're disgusting health

hazards, just like all three of you." She slammed the wad of paper on my desk and wheeled around.

Barely moving a prehistoric muscle, Mr. Downer rapped a ruler against his desk. "Mr. Morelli and Ms. Hopkins," he said. "You are excused from this class."

"Me?" said Valerie. "Why am I in trouble? *He's* the one throwing trash around the room."

"You caused the disruption. So you're excused. Maybe Mr. Groton will see it differently."

I packed my bag and stood up.

Fish leaned over and smiled. "Dude," he said.

"Yeah?"

"I don't think you're going to make it to batting practice."

Valerie and I got to the door at the same time. She made a big scene about going through it first, then pushing it shut in my face. Out in the hallway, I walked a few steps behind her. "Can you believe that guy?" I asked her. "One little incident and he throws us out of class." Valerie sped up, but I kept talking. "We should form a club for people who hate Mr. Downer."

"You don't get to talk to me," Valerie said without looking back.

"You're mad at me," I said. "I can tell. But if we keep our cool and work together, we can get out of this."

She spun around. "Did I not make myself clear, Health Hazard? I don't want you talking to me. I'm supposed to go to a meeting this afternoon to start planning the graduation party and I don't want to be late. So *shut* it."

That wasn't exactly what I meant by working together. But the way she pretended not to like me was intoxicating. "You know, someday we'll probably laugh about this. Maybe over a slice of pizza. My treat."

She didn't even bother to slow down. It went on like that all the way to the principal's office, where she sat next to me, facing the window with her arms crossed.

Mr. Groton eyed us from behind his desk for a minute or two. First me, then Valerie, then me again. Was he waiting for one of us to break? "Does someone want to tell me what happened?" he finally asked. "Valerie?"

"It's not my fault," she said. I knew she was mad, but her cheeks were as red as apples and she looked even prettier than usual.

Mr. Groton looked at me. "Roy?"

After thinking about it, I decided to take the heat. I figured I would be like the knight in shining armor, saving the day for Valerie. So I said, "It was all my fault, Mr. Groton. Valerie had nothing to do with it."

"Are you sure?" Mr. Groton asked.

"I'm sure."

Mr. Groton looked at Valerie. "Is this true? Mr. Downer said you caused quite a disturbance."

"I was upset because Roy had thrown some trash

into my bag. I may have overreacted. But I don't think I should be punished for it."

Apparently, Mr. Groton agreed. He sent Valerie back to class. Then he made me sit there while he called Mom. And that was when I knew I was *really* in trouble.

· 6 ·

Mom went bananas as soon as I had buckled my seat belt. She sped through town like she was fleeing the scene of a crime. "I have *one* hour between work and class," she said to me. "*One* hour. Do you think I want to spend that hour picking you up from the principal's office?"

"It was a misunderstanding," I said. I had never seen her this mad at anyone besides Dad. And that was in the middle of the divorce.

"You had a bag over your head," she said. "In class."

"Okay, okay, it got a little out of hand. But it won't happen again. I promise."

"I also talked to your teacher," she said after a minute.

"Which one?" I asked, even though I knew who it was.

"Mr. Downing," she said.

"Downer," I muttered.

"What?"

"Downer," I told her. "His name is Mr. Downer."

Mom's knuckles went white on the steering wheel. "Roy," she said. "How could you let things get this bad?"

"I didn't mean to," I said.

Mom came to a screeching halt at a stop sign. "He told me you got a thirty-seven on your last test. He said you have a D average, Roy. A *D*! I can't believe it. All those times I thought you were reading, you weren't, were you?"

A car honked behind us. We were still at the stop sign.

"And when I asked you the other day if you knew your grade, you did, didn't you?" The car honked again.

"I'm *going*," Mom said into the rearview mirror. She gunned the car forward. "You lied to me, Roy."

"I'm sorry."

"Did you really think I wouldn't find out?"

"I'll do better," I promised.

Mom turned and looked at me, even though she was driving down a narrow street with cars parked on both sides of the road. "When?" she asked. "When baseball season starts?" Her eyes momentarily went back on the road. We were in the right lane. Up ahead was a parked car. Mom turned to me again. "Why would I believe anything is going to change because of this conversation?"

I wasn't sure whether to answer the question, or tell her about the parked car we were about to hit. Both seemed to be dangerous. The car was coming up fast. Mom kept going. I leaned back in my seat, bracing for impact.

"Huh?" she asked. "I'm waiting."

"Car," I said, pointing forward.

Without taking her eyes off me, Mom changed lanes. "I want an answer, Roy."

"I don't know what you want me to say."

"Give me one reason to believe things are going to change at school," said Mom.

"I can't," I said.

"Then I'll give you a reason," Mom said, pulling the car to the side of the road. She took a deep breath. "You're not going to play on the All-Star team this season."

I shot forward so fast that the seat belt snapped tight against my shoulder. "But that's my team!" I yelped. "The season starts tomorrow. I can't quit now. They're counting on me."

"Not this year, Roy" she said, shutting off the car's engine.

"You don't understand, Mom. I *have* to be on the All-Star team this season. My future depends on it."

Mom shook her head. "No, *you* don't get it, Roy. Your future depends on school. Not baseball."

"So what are you saying?" I asked. "I can't play baseball?"

"You can play with Fish and Kenny."

"What! In the rec league?"

"What's wrong with the rec league?" Mom asked.

"I might as well go back to T-ball!" I told her. "You know you're not even allowed to *steal* in that league? They only practice once a week!"

"Exactly," said Mom.

"But—"

"Take the deal, Roy. Because it's the best I have to offer."

"The rec league?" I repeated.

Mom started up the car again. "Or no league. You choose."

We didn't speak the rest of the way home. I sat in my seat, my fists clenched tightly. I felt like I had hit a cartoon wall. The road ahead had seemed so clear. Finish eighth grade. Be the big dog in the All-Star League. Play shortstop for Coach Harden next spring. And then in a split second . . . BAM!!! I was lying in the middle of the road with birds chirping over my head because someone had painted yellow lines and pavement on the side of a mountain.

When we got to the house, Mom pulled up to the curb. "I have to go to class," she said. "Your father will pick you up here for the weekend."

"Does he know?" I asked, unbuckling my seat belt.

Mom shook her head. "I got his voice mail."

"Roy," Mom said as I got out of the car. "This isn't the end of the world."

Maybe not, but it felt like it. I needed to be on that team. I needed to impress Coach Harden. How was I supposed to do that playing in the rec league? I glanced at Mom. She didn't get it.

But Dad would.

• 7 •

It was a nice night, so after dinner, Sara, Dad, and I walked down the street to the small park at the end of the block. Sara was trailing, leaving me alone with Dad. I had been waiting for the right time to have a man-to-man chat. I wanted him to talk to Mom. He knew all about the All-Star team. All about Coach Harden. He knew what it meant to be one of Bull Harden's prospects. He could make her see why it was so important.

"Can we talk?" I asked Dad.

"Sure," he said. "I want to talk to you too."

I spoke quickly, rushing to get it all out before Sara caught up with us. "Mom says I can't play on the All-Star team. But she doesn't understand. She doesn't know about Coach Harden. And this poseur Moochie is gunning for my spot. Can you talk to her?"

"I already did," Dad said, switching the basketball from one hand to the other.

Excited, I hit the brakes. "So I can play?"

"Roy, I agree with your mother."

"You what?"

"I agree with your mother. You need to focus on your grades. I know this is a shock to you. We're partly to blame for that. Neither of us realized how far things had sunk at school. But we're all in this together now. You're going to do better at school. You're going to get back on track. And when you do, baseball will still be there."

"Not if I don't play on the All-Star team!" I said, raising my voice so Dad would get it.

"Watch it, Roy," he said. "This isn't the ball field and we're not joking around now. I'm your father and I'm telling you school comes first."

"Fine," I said more calmly. "School comes first. I'll try harder. But you have to let me play on the All-Stars. If I don't, I might not make the high school team."

"Listen to me," Dad snapped. "If you don't deal with this *right now*, not playing high school baseball is going to be the least of your problems."

"It's just one D," I said, pressing my palms against the basketball.

"Your mom also said you lied to her when she asked you about the test. Is that true?"

"I guess. But I said I was sorry."

"Apologizing isn't enough," Dad said. "We have to deal with this, and deal with it now. Just like when you were learning to hit and you had a hitch in your swing. Remember? You dropped your elbow every time. Your coach and I worked hard to correct it early because we knew how hard it would be to break the habit later. This D is the hitch in your swing. We gotta fix it before it leads to big problems later."

"Okay," I grumbled as we approached the park.

It was just a small grassy area, a playground, and a concrete court with two hoops. When Sara caught up with us, she took one look around, grabbed a seat on a bench, and whipped out her phone.

"There *is* some good news," Dad said as we walked toward the court. "You're getting B's and C's in your other classes. If you can get that history grade up, you'll be at your eighth grade graduation before you know it. Maybe you'll turn some of those C's into B's while you're at it."

"How is that good news? History is my worst class."

"Well, I think I know someone who can help you. She's a history teacher. She tutors at the library in town."

We were facing each other now. "Who?"

"Camille."

Dad tossed me the ball, but I couldn't concentrate and it bounced off my hands.

I held the ball with two hands. "How does she know about my grades? Did you tell her?"

"No," said Dad. "But I know she'd help."

"Do I have to?"

"Not yet," he said. "But you're on a short leash, pal. We want to see improvement. If we don't, you may not have a choice." He pointed to the ball. "Now, are you going to check that or not?"

For the next ten minutes, we played an easy game of one-on-one. We stuck mostly to outside shots. Dad got hot and knocked down a few jumpers. My game was off. I never got going. Before long, Dad was up 8–2 in a game to 11. He finished me off with a bank shot, a layin, and a fadeaway.

Then he looked over at Sara. She was camped on the bench, just spaced out with her arms crossed. "Hey, you!" Dad called. "You want in? Your brother needs help."

"No thanks," she said.

Dad flipped me the ball. He walked over to the bench. Then he sat down next to Sara. He crossed his arms, scowled, and pretended to twirl his hair.

"Stop it," said Sara.

I laughed.

"It's not funny," she said. But she was cracking. Pretty soon she couldn't help it. She was biting her lip to keep from smiling. Finally, she turned and gave Dad a playful shove. "I can't believe you're making fun of your own daughter."

Dad stood up and faced the bench. "Come play with us," he said, offering Sara his hand. "Just one game."

"Fine," said Sara. "*One* game."

Dad raised his hands in the air. "Okay!" he said. "That's more like it. The Morellis take the court!"

Music began to play in the pocket of Sara's sweatshirt. She stopped in her tracks and drew out her phone. I saw Dad's face fall. "Sara," he called, "put the phone away and . . ." But Sara was already gone, and Dad and I were alone on the court.

We shot around for a bit, then Sara joined us on one of the picnic tables and watched the sun set. "So who's the girl?" Dad asked me.

"What girl?" Sara said, suddenly interested again.

"Your mom says Roy brought a date to the principal's office."

"That was no date," I said. "That was Valerie, from my history class. We had a misunderstanding."

"Do you like her?" Dad asked.

"Depends what you mean by *like*."

"If you like her, you should ask her on a date," said Dad.

"I tried that. It didn't go over too well." I didn't mention that we were on our way to the principal's office at the time.

Sara pulled her hands into her sleeves. "Well, whatever you do, don't call it a date. Just ask her if she wants to go hang out. That way she can say no without rejecting you. She doesn't have to feel sorry for you and you don't have to go to school the next day knowing that she knows that you like her. Everyone wins."

"That's pretty complicated," said Dad.

"Not as complicated as history," I said.

Later that evening, I called Fish and Kenny and invited them to come over and watch basketball. I felt bad about not going to the market with them. When they showed up at the apartment, Sara was on the phone and Dad was in the big brown armchair with his history book. Fish gave me a look as he walked through the front door.

"What's with you?" I asked.

"Nothing," he said. "I'm just surprised you called. I thought you'd be too busy with the All-Star team."

"I told you I was sorry about that," I said, following them into the TV room. "It was a last-minute thing. Anyway, I didn't even get to go with them."

"What do you mean?" Kenny asked.

I told them what had happened.

"So you're not gonna play baseball?" Fish asked as he took a seat on the end of the couch. I sat on the other end and Kenny took the middle.

"Not for the All-Star team."

"What about Coach Harden? I thought you were his top prospect."

"You don't have to rub it in," I said. "My baseball career is finished."

"You're washed up," Fish agreed.

"I know."

"A has-been."

"Thanks."

"A never-was."

I reached over Kenny and punched Fish in the shoulder. Fish socked me back.

"What am I going to do?" I asked, slumping back on the couch.

"You could play with us," said Kenny. "It could be fun. The three of us on the field together again."

"I don't know if that's a good idea," I said. "It's not really my league."

"It's still baseball," Kenny said.

We both looked down the couch at Fish as he knocked back his soda, turned the can upside down, then belched. "What?" he asked.

"We want to know what you think," Kenny said.

Fish stared at the game. "About what?"

"About Roy playing on our team."

"You're not going to ditch us again, are you?"

"I didn't *ditch* you," I said. "It was a change of plans. And, no, I wouldn't ditch you."

Fish shrugged. "Then play with us. Or don't. What do I care?"

"I'll think about it," I promised.

The game ended around ten. As they were leaving, Kenny turned to me. "If you decide to come, our first practice is tomorrow at two o'clock on Field Seven at Boardman Park."

Fish and I shoved each other as he walked out the door. "It would be kinda cool," he said. Then he belched again. "Thanks for the soda."

"I need oxygen," I said, waving my hand in front of my face.

After they were gone, I started thinking it would be fun to be on the same team as them again. Playing in the rec league would be a walk in the park for me, and the guys would probably pay money to learn a few things from an All-Star. I'd be like a human instructional video. But then again, it wasn't my league.

I found Dad asleep in the chair. *The People's History of the United States* was open and lying on his chest. We were definitely related.

He stirred when I walked into the room.

"How you doing?" he asked, sitting up.

"I'd be better if I could play on the All-Star team."

"You want my advice?" Dad said. "Listen to your mother. Play with Kenny and Fish. I know it's not the All-Stars, but it's still baseball. Go out there and have a good time. Enjoy the game. Make some new friends."

"The rec league . . . ," I said. "It's like the All-Star League with training wheels. Do you know what that could do to my skills?"

"I know it stinks, but it's the best option you have. I'm saying you should take it. The worst thing you can do at a time like this is feel sorry for yourself. Trust me. Besides, there's no rule that says you can't play your best."

Maybe, I thought as I got ready for bed, but what good was my best if nobody was there to see it?

· 8 ·

I didn't even want to leave the apartment on Saturday morning. But I had to break the news to Coach Burke and the rest of the All-Star team. So after breakfast, I dragged myself down to Boardman Park. Practice started at one o'clock, but I got to the park at twelve-thirty, hoping to catch Ruben or Derek heading in early. They could pass along the message. It would be less painful that way.

But the only person I saw was Coach Harden. He was sitting on a bench outside the grandstand, reading a newspaper.

He looked up as I came around the corner.

The white hair under his hat and the wrinkles across his suntanned face made him look old enough to be my grandfather—but with the forearms to throw a baseball flatfooted from home plate to the parking lot.

It was no wonder he was a legend. And I was going to make sure he always remembered the day he met Roy Morelli.

"You're not dressed for practice," he said.

I looked down at my jeans and sneakers. "I can't play this season because of grades," I said. "But I'm going to be on the high school team next year."

"You are, huh? You think you're ready?"

"I'm ready, sir," I said, looking him in the eye. "I hit .387 last season. I led the league in home runs and stolen bases. I get to first base faster than most lefties and can throw a runner out from my knees."

"I see," said Coach, folding his newspaper.

"So you think I'm good enough?" I asked.

"It sounds like you've got the five tools." He raised each finger on his left hand one at a time and said, "Average, power, fielding, speed, and arm strength. But there's a sixth tool."

"There is?"

He tapped the side of his head. "Your mental game," he said. "Your brain is a muscle, and it's just as important as your legs and arms. So make sure you use it."

"I will, sir. I promise."

Coach nodded and smiled. "It's too bad you can't play All-Star ball this spring. I saw you last weekend at the workout. I liked what I saw."

I liked what I saw. The words every prospect wanted to hear. It made me feel alive again. Still, I had to play it cool. "You were there?" I asked, trying to sound breezy.

"You waved to me," said Coach.

"Right."

A moment passed. Then Coach asked, "So what *are* your plans this spring?"

"You mean baseball?" I asked.

He nodded.

"It's rec league or no league," I said.

Coach took a sip of his coffee. "Sounds like a no-brainer."

And suddenly it *was* a no-brainer. If spending a season in the rec league was what I had to do, then I would spend a season in the rec league. How bad could it be?

Just then, voices drifted across the park. They were coming our way. That was when Coach stood up. He folded his paper under his arm. "That's my cue," he said. He walked toward the entrance of the grandstand, then stopped. "I don't normally get to many rec league games. But I do make exceptions. You show me something this season and there might be a spot for you on my team next year." Then he gave me a wink and added, "I'll be watching, Roy. Impress me."

I stood in front of the grandstand, feeling like the king of Pilchuck. Impress him? I was going to *dazzle* him. I was going to leave him rubbing his eyes. By the time I was done, he'd have *Did I Just See That?* plastered across his face in letters so big I could see it from home plate.

The voices that had sent Coach Harden packing drew closer. I could tell now it was Ruben and Derek.

"Morelli," Ruben said when he saw me. "What's with the jeans?"

"Yeah," Derek said. "You stash your stuff somewhere?"

I shook my head. "I'm out," I said. "You're gonna have to get by without me this season." I told them about my grades and about the rec league. But I left out the part about Coach Harden.

"Tough break," Derek said.

I felt bad about letting them down. "You'll manage."

Derek gave me a look. "I mean, for you."

Ruben held out his hand. "Come see us sometime."

"I'll try," I said, slapping his hand. "I'm going to be pretty busy with games and practices."

"Take it easy, Morelli," Ruben said with a nod. Then he and Derek disappeared into the grandstand. They seemed to take it better than I thought they would, or maybe they just didn't want to show how much they were going to miss me.

Later that afternoon, I caught up with Fish and Kenny on the path that cut between the ball fields by the grandstand. I got right to the point. "I'm in," I said. "I'm going to play with you guys."

"Awesome," Kenny said, pumping his fist.

Fish was still playing it cool. "I don't know about this."

"Are you kidding me?" I asked. I wished he would drop the act. After all, I was the victim here, not him.

Kenny turned to Fish. "We do need one more guy," he said. "Andy dropped out to play soccer."

"He should know what he's getting into," Fish said to Kenny.

"What?" I asked. "What do I need to know?"

"Tell him," said Fish.

"Tell me what?"

Kenny took a deep breath. "Our team isn't very good, Roy."

"So you're not league champs. I just want to play baseball. I don't care about records."

"We won one game last year," Kenny said. "And that was by forfeit. The other team didn't show up."

"Then you have nowhere to go but up," I said. "I don't see what the problem is." True, a one-win season was not very good, but with my help, we could go from worst to first—and if Coach Harden was paying attention, he'd have to be impressed by *that*.

"Okay," Fish said, with his hand out. "If this is what you want. Just remember, whatever happens, don't say we didn't warn you."

"Nothing's gonna happen," I said, placing my hand on his. "Trust me, I don't care how bad your team is."

"You're not the only one," Kenny muttered, laying his hand on top of mine.

Kenny and I continued walking across the field, but Fish stopped to talk to a group of guys I didn't know.

"Who are they?" I asked Kenny when we were in the dugout, which had a cement floor, wood ceiling, and a chain-link fence for walls.

"That's Julian," said Kenny, pointing to the taller one. "The guy with the red hair is Shane, and that's Luther standing next to him. They all go to Parkside."

I saw Wyatt pass in front of them. Julian said something and they all started laughing. Ignoring them, Wyatt joined McKlusky, who had been standing by himself in the outfield.

Then I noticed someone standing alone on the mound, like he was just waiting for a batter to show up. "Who's the pitcher?" I asked.

"Don't know," said Kenny. "He's new. He must go to Parkside, too."

After I had laced up my cleats, someone else walked into the dugout. I thought he might be someone's dad. He was kind of goofy-looking. His shirt was tucked in too tight and his pants fell a little short of his shoes.

"Hi there," he said to me. "I'm Coach Darby."

"Roy Morelli," I told him. I wondered if he had heard of me.

Coach Darby unfolded a piece of paper. "I don't see your name on the roster, Roy."

"I haven't actually signed up yet," I explained. "This was kind of a last-minute decision."

"Have you played baseball before?" he asked.

I guess he *hadn't* heard of me.

"Not in this league. I was on the All-Star team."

Coach Darby smiled. "Well, everyone's welcome in the rec league," he said, like that was something special. Then he walked over to third base and waved the team in from the field. It took a while. Some of the guys were too busy tackling each other. Coach Darby had to call three times. He never got mad, though. I tried to imagine Coach Harden or Coach Burke waiting patiently like that.

When he finally had everyone's attention, Coach Darby spoke. "Welcome back!" he said, spreading his arms wide. We were standing in a circle and he was in the middle. "It's good to see so many familiar faces— and a couple of new ones." He looked at me and the pitcher. "For those of you who don't know, I've been a volunteer coach for twenty years—since my own kids were in the rec league. They're all grown up now, but I keep coaching. My goal is for everyone to enjoy the game of baseball, no matter what their skill level is."

On the other side of the circle, I saw Luther whisper to Julian.

"Luther," said Coach Darby. "I need you and Julian to focus for another minute, then we can play ball."

"Who's the new guy?" Julian asked.

"This is Caleb," said Coach. "And—"

"We know Caleb from school," said Shane. "Who's the other guy?" He pointed at me.

I looked over at Fish, but he wasn't making eye contact. "My name is Roy," I told Shane, beating Coach to the punch. "Roy Morelli."

"He goes to Pilchuck with us," said Kenny. "He used to play on the All-Star team."

"Oooh," said Julian, shaking his hands. "I'm so impressed. I've never seen an All-Star up close before."

"I'm not surprised," I said, to let him know I didn't like being messed with.

We were talking past Coach Darby now. Like it was monkey in the middle and he was it.

Julian stared at me. "You're not better than us."

"Did someone say I was?" I asked.

Coach Darby held up his hands. "Okay, okay. Nobody here is any better or worse than anyone else," he said.

What a bunch of garbage. How could nine guys on a team be exactly the same?

But Coach wasn't done. "Who remembers what my only rule is?" he asked. He held up one finger and walked around the circle. Nobody had a guess, so he said, "Have fun! The important thing to remember is that we can have a good time whether we win or lose. If we work hard, play our best, and appreciate each other, we'll have fun no matter what the scoreboard says."

"Why even keep score?" I mumbled under my breath. Only someone who had never won anything could say the scoreboard didn't matter.

Next Coach Darby told us we were going to start with fielding practice. But he forgot to assign us positions.

I went to shortstop . . . along with most of the team.

"Don't you think we should take *different* positions?" I asked.

"What's the point?" Shane asked. "Coach Darby only hits the ball in one direction."

Coach Darby held a bat in one hand and a baseball in the other hand. "Ready?" he called.

"Ready!" a few people shouted.

"Here she comes." Coach Darby tossed the ball in the air and nearly swung himself out of his shoes.

"Strike one!" a couple of the guys yelled.

"Okay," Coach Darby called back. "I'm just a little rusty. I'll get this one."

He tossed the ball a little higher. But he swung too early.

"Strike two!" Louder this time.

Coach Darby blushed a bit. "Okay, okay," he said. "Just be patient with me."

Patient? This guy was supposed to be a coach. How

were we supposed to get anywhere learning baseball from someone who couldn't even pitch to himself?

Coach Darby got a piece of the next ball. It dribbled about four feet from the plate and died on the dirt. That didn't stop Julian, Shane, and McKlusky from chasing it down like dogs going after a tennis ball. I was surprised to see Fish throw himself on top of the pile. Was this how he thought the team was going to get better?

After three more grounders, I turned to Kenny. "Does he ever hit anything decent?" I asked.

Kenny shrugged. "Not really."

I stayed in place, feeling a little queasy. Coach Darby struck himself out two more times before I decided I had seen enough. I slid my glove off my hand and walked up to the plate. "Can I try?" I asked.

He smiled. "Well, I'm not sure that would be fair, Roy. If I give you a turn, I'm going to have to give everyone a turn."

If he *didn't* give me a turn, we were going to spend the whole practice watching him whiff at his own pitches.

"Everyone can have a turn," I promised. "Just let me go first." I held my hand out for the bat.

"I suppose it can't hurt," said Coach, offering me the bat.

But as soon as I grabbed it, there was a cry from the outfield. "How come Roy gets to hit?" yelled Luther.

Shane jogged in from third base. "I call next," he said.

Julian sped after him. "I call third."

"Fourth!" Luther shouted.

McKlusky was next. "Fifth!" he yelled, taking the glove off his left hand.

Then Fish. "Sixth!"

And Kenny. "Seventh!"

"Eighth!" said Caleb, running in from the outfield.

Wyatt came in last. "Ninth," he said.

Julian cupped his finger to his ear. "Did someone say something?" he asked.

"Ninth," Wyatt repeated a little louder. He looked mad and embarrassed at the same time. But seeing Wyatt turn red just made Julian and Shane crack up.

"Boys," said Coach Darby. "Is there something you'd like to say?"

Julian stopped laughing. "Yeah, can we hit now?"

"Yeah," Shane said. "Fielding is boring."

"Fielding isn't boring," I told him. "It's the most important part of baseball."

The other guys were facing me. They stood in small groups. Kenny was to my left with Wyatt, Caleb, and McKlusky close by. To my right, Julian, Shane, and Luther had their arms crossed and were glaring at me. Fish was a few feet away from them.

"Let's all go back to the field for a few more minutes," said Coach Darby. "Then we can hit."

There was a lot of griping from the guys as they realized we weren't going to hit yet. I found a spot in shallow left, where I stood in the grass waiting for something to come my way. But Coach Darby never even got a ball out of the infield.

· 9 ·

On Tuesday night, I was in the living room watching the Mariners and the Twins when Mom came home from class. "Roy," she said as soon as she saw me, "why are you watching television?"

"I was just taking a break," I said, holding up my history book. A pile of crumbs fell on the carpet.

"I thought your father and I made it clear that you need to be focusing on your grades, not on baseball."

"I can't even *watch* baseball?"

"Turn it off and go to your room," said Mom. "You have homework to do."

I pushed myself up from the couch and went to my room. But when I started reading a chapter of history, nothing stuck. I tried to answer the questions in the practice quiz at the end of the chapter and got them all wrong. Frustrated, I flipped the book shut and found the game on the radio. I'd worry about history later.

On Wednesday afternoon, I went with Fish and Kenny to Pilchuck Market. I was hoping to run into Valerie. I thought she might want to thank me for saving her in Mr. Groton's office.

"We can't stay too long," Kenny said. "Practice starts in an hour."

"Relax," I said. "This'll only take a minute."

I spotted Valerie inside the store. She was in line—fifth from the register. Bingo.

"There she is," I said. "Time to work my magic."

"Never gonna happen," said Fish.

"Trust me," I said. "I'm wearing her down. It's like fighting off strikes. Pretty soon I'm going to connect."

"Maybe you should just be friends with her," Kenny suggested.

"Friends?" I said. "What's the point of that? I have enough friends already. If I want another friend, I'll get a dog."

"You should try that line on Valerie," Fish said, shaking his head. "I'm sure that will melt her heart."

I pushed my way into the crowded store, grabbed a candy bar, and sidestepped a few people until Valerie was right in front of me. She was holding a bottle of water. "How about a candy bar to go with that?" I said.

"No thanks," she said, barely turning around. "I'm not hungry."

"It's for me," I said. "It's my way of saying you're welcome."

Valerie narrowed her eyes. "I'm *welcome*? What have you ever done for me?"

"I got you out of Mr. Groton's office."

"You got me *into* Mr. Groton's office!" She shook her head. "Ugh. Why am I even talking to you?"

Valerie was at the register now. I had to act fast!

"Okay, okay," I said to the back of her neck. "Forget the candy bar. I don't like chocolate anyway. How about if we get some pizza Friday? You like pepperoni?"

I hadn't forgotten what happened the last time I asked Valerie to go for pizza, but I wasn't going to give up that easily.

"Would you go out with someone who got you in trouble? Someone who harassed you at school? Someone who *embarrassed* you in front of your friends?" She held up her hand. "Don't answer that yet," she told me. Then she said, loud enough for everyone in Pilchuck to hear, "Roy Morelli, I would not go for pizza with you if we were the last two people on earth *and you paid*."

Everyone around us laughed.

Fish shook his head in disgust. Kenny couldn't even look at me. I was all alone.

It was like having someone run my underwear up the flagpole without letting me take them off first. "That was cold," I said.

Valerie leaned in. "Still wanna go for pizza?" she asked. Then she left me in the dust, right out in the open for everyone to see.

"Dee-nied!" I heard someone say.

"I don't think she likes you, dude," said someone else.

There was no doubt about that now. I had lost a month of my life chasing after this girl. Well, never again! I had always thought it was a good thing that Valerie told it like it was. And now I could see her for what *she* was—a stuck-up, heartless, ungrateful waste of my time. She should want to be seen with *me* in the hallway, not the other way around.

My face was still burning as Fish, Kenny, and I hurried away from the store. I needed to get as far away from Valerie as I could. Like the North Pole. But since I didn't have a dog sled, Boardman Park would have to do.

"Forget about her, man," Fish said as we jogged down a side street. "Girls are nothing but trouble."

"Yeah," Kenny said between breaths. "We're better off on our own."

"Thanks," I said. "I was pretty much over her anyway." I had to agree with them. Girls were a hassle.

All I wanted to do was get on the field, where it was just a group of guys bashing a ball with a bat. Well, we hadn't gotten to do any bashing last week, but I was sure we would today. After all, the first game was just four days away.

But when it was time to take the field, Coach Darby was holding the bat.

"Let's do some fielding!" he said, like it was the greatest idea in the world.

Getting more bent out of shape by the second, I ran to shortstop. If I wasn't going to hit a ball, at least I could throw one—hard. Sometimes hearing the *whup* of the baseball hitting the leather of a glove was all it took to feel better.

"Ready, Roy?" Coach called, pointing the bat at me.

"Ready," I said, bending my knees.

Coach hit a grounder right toward me. I charged the ball, got it in my hand, and set my feet. With all my might, I hurled it across the infield at Luther, who was playing first base.

But the ball didn't make a *whup* when it hit his glove; it made a *WHAP!* as Luther's whole left arm snapped backward.

"Yeow!" he shouted, taking the glove off. "That stung." He looked over at Coach. "Can you tell the new guy not to throw so hard? It's just practice."

I hoped Coach would tell Luther that practices were supposed to get us ready for games, and that when it mattered, nobody was going to take it easy. But instead, Coach said, "Hey, Roy, nice and easy now. We're just having fun here, okay?"

Speak for yourself Coach, I thought. Now how was I going to blow off steam? I couldn't throw hard. And there was no chance to hit. We spent the second half of practice fighting over shirt numbers until it was time to go.

I stayed on the empty field and threw a baseball against the backstop. It was dark by the time I quit. By then, my arm hurt, but everything else felt a little better.

• 10 •

Friday finally rolled around. The week was almost over, but it felt like history class would never end.

I hadn't done the reading last night. I knew if I brought home another bad grade, it would land me in tutoring sessions with Camille. But there were still two weeks until the next test. I'd be able to come up with something between now and then.

I drooped into my seat and tried to stay awake. I was drifting off when Derek kicked the back of my chair. "Hey, Morelli," he said. "How's life in the minor leagues?" He was wearing a fitted blue cap with a big *P* on the front.

"Too soon to tell," I said over my shoulder. "We've only had two practices. Ask me again next week."

Derek kicked the chair again. "Don't you want to know about Moochie?" he asked.

"Stop," said Mr. Downer. I looked up. I thought he might be talking to me and Derek. But he pointed at Emily and said, "Read."

"Moochie's a bum. I'm not worried about him."

"Well, that bum hit one over the wall in practice this week. Right in front of Coach Harden."

I clenched my fists. I hoped Mom and Dad were happy. Thanks to them, my one chance at greatness was slipping away. And for what? How was playing in the rec league supposed to help me in school? It didn't make this boring class any less boring. It didn't make Mr. Downer a better teacher. All it did was punish me for no good reason.

Mr. Downer rocked forward. "Stop," he said to Emily, before looking at Raj. "Begin reading."

Fish leaned over. "We need a new game."

"Thumb war?" Kenny asked.

"No thumb war," I told them. "I've got a better idea." I reached into my book bag. I found a paper clip and twisted it into a hook.

I listened long enough to hear Raj say, "The Treaty of Guadalupe Hildago . . . ," then went back to work. I undid one lace and tied it to the paper clip. "Let's go fishing."

"For what?" asked Kenny.

"Whatever we can catch," I said.

"Is this even a game?" asked Fish. "How do you win?"

"Catch the biggest fish," I said, making it up as I went.

Fish shrugged. "Beats history," he said, taking the shoelace. He gathered up a bit of the slack, then pitched the paper clip forward. He was aiming for the backpack on the floor next to Wyatt's desk, but the paper clip fell short. "Do-over," he said. He pinched the end of the lace and threw it over his shoulder, like he was casting.

A second later, we heard Ruben say, "Watch it, Fishman." He flung the paper clip back at Fish, then popped him once in the shoulder.

"Gimme that," I said to Fish. "If we were stuck on an island, you'd starve."

I looked around the room for a target as Raj finished reading. I waited, in case Mr. Downer called on me. Instead, he pointed at Valerie—my new enemy.

Perfect, I thought, spying a small purple spiral notebook sticking out of her half-open bag. I licked my pointer finger, tested the wind, and went fishing.

". . . fifty-four forty or fight," Valerie was reading, when the hook hit the edge of the notebook. I pulled up gently. Suddenly, I had the notebook by the spiral. I began reeling it in, silently, so she wouldn't look down.

The clock was ticking.

"Better hurry," said Kenny.

The notebook cleared the top of the bag. That was when I got cocky. I gave it a tug and it fell to the floor.

Valerie stopped mid-sentence. She looked down and saw her notebook on the end of my line. "You have got to be joking," she said, in a rage. She leapt to her feet, grabbed the notebook with both hands, and yanked—hard. The string flew out of my hand.

"Ms. Hopkins," Mr. Downer barked. "Pack your things and go see Mr. Groton. This is the last time you disrupt my class."

"What about *him*? He tried to steal my notebook."

"Roy can pick up where you left off," said Mr. Downer.

Valerie hurled a book into her bag. "This is so unfair!"

Mr. Downer ignored her. "Mr. Morelli," he said calmly. "Please show the class how well you've been paying attention. Begin reading where Valerie stopped."

I scrambled to find the right place in the book. "The Gadsden Purchase . . . ," I began.

"No," said Mr. Downer. "Next page."

Moving my finger to the next section break, I tried again. "The Kansas-Nebraska Bill . . ."

"No," Mr. Downer said. "That's too far."

Kenny tapped the right spot in his book.

"Sorry, Mr. Downer," I said. I went to the spot Kenny had shown me and started, "The Fugitive Slave Act . . ." I paused, waiting to be interrupted, but Mr.

Downer was hibernating again, so I kept going. Two minutes later, my turn was over. Kenny and Fish were in a thumb war. "I got next," I whispered.

Sara made dinner that night. Mac 'n' cheese with peas and salad out of a bag. After dinner, I joined her in the living room. I figured if she could study with the TV on, maybe it would work for me too. I hadn't gotten very far when the front door squeaked open and keys fell on the counter. The clock above the TV said 7:03. Heels clicked on the linoleum. They were headed my way.

Sara looked up from her book. "Mom's early," she said. "And you're dead meat."

"I'm doing my homework, same as you."

"Then how come you haven't turned a page since you sat down?"

Sara was right, I thought, as Mom came into the living room. I was toast.

Sara scooped up her books like the house was on fire. "See ya," she said to me. She passed Mom on the way to the kitchen. "How was class?"

"Fine, sweetie," Mom said. "Thank you for asking."

"Yeah, you're a real angel," I said, but Sara ignored me.

Mom glared at me when we were alone. "Turn off the television, Roy."

I hit the mute button. "I know, I'm in the living

room. But I was doing my homework." Mom didn't say anything. "You let Sara study with the TV on."

"*Off,*" she said, snatching the remote from my hand. "Your teacher called."

"*Again?* I can't believe that guy."

Suddenly Mom came down on me like an avalanche. "Roy, what is going on in your head?" she barked, her voice rumbling with anger. "Your father and I tell you to start taking school seriously and this is what we get? We wanted to see a change. But nothing has changed."

"Something has changed," I said. "I'm not on the All-Star team."

Mom coughed in disbelief. "You think that's what this is about? *Baseball?* This is about your life, Roy—and how you choose to lead it." She jabbed her finger at me. "We gave you a chance to show us that you could take responsibility on your own. But you decided not to do that. So I'm going to make the decision for you."

What else was there? "I don't have to quit the rec league, too, do I?"

"If it was up to me . . ." She shook her head. "No, you're not going to quit baseball. But you are going to start tutoring."

"Where?"

"At the library," she said. "With . . . Camille."

"You know about that?"

"Your dad told me. Look, Roy. I'm still getting used

to this situation too. And it isn't easy for me either. But I do not have the time to hold your hand anymore. I have to think about the future—for all of us. So until I can trust you to do the right thing on your own, this is what has to happen."

"Just give me one more chance," I said.

"Roy Morelli, you are out of chances. Mr. Downer said you have two weeks until your next test. It's time for you to step up to the plate."

· 11 ·

Dad drove me from Mom's house to the game on Saturday. We were playing the Dodgers. "You're kinda quiet, pal," he said. "It's the first day of baseball season. I thought you'd be excited."

I looked down at my new uniform—a pair of pants that didn't fit right and a T-shirt with *Pirates* written across the front in iron-on letters. I missed the button-down jerseys from the All-Star team.

"Yeah," I said to Dad. "I'm really psyched."

"This isn't about baseball, is it?" he asked. "Look, pal, when we said you needed to focus on school this spring, there was more to it than switching baseball teams. You have work to do. And you can't do it alone. If you don't want to work with Camille, that's fine. Maybe your teacher can spend some time with you after class."

"Those are my choices?" I said. "That's worse than rec league or no league."

"Come on, Roy. Don't feel sorry for yourself. Focus on the game today. Be positive. No scout wants to see his prospect mope around the field for seven innings. Go out there and play baseball the way you know how. *That* will impress Coach Harden."

But when I walked to the maple tree near the third baseline and scanned the four rows of bleachers for Coach Harden, there was no sign of him. Just then Coach Darby approached, holding a clipboard. He was probably making up the batting order. I wasn't sure if he'd have me bat first because I could get on base—or fourth because I had power.

"Where do I bat?" I asked.

Coach looked confused. "You bat right over there at the plate," he said.

"No," I said. "I mean, where do I bat in the lineup? Leadoff? Cleanup? Either one is fine. I can hit for average or power, so . . ."

After checking the clipboard, Coach said, "Roy, you're batting sixth today. Next week we'll change it. That way everyone gets the same number of at bats this season."

"Don't you want the best hitters at the top of the lineup so they get up more?" I asked. But Coach was already on his way to the dugout.

"Batting sixth, that's gotta be rough."

I turned around to see Moochie Goodman. He was wearing blue and gold track pants and his fitted hat with the All-Star emblem on the side. I wanted to snatch the hat from his head and swat him with it. "What do you want, Moochie?"

"Just checking out the talent," he said, gesturing to my teammates on the field. "If you can call this talent."

"They're good enough for me," I said.

"You better hope these guys are better than *good enough* if you want to impress Coach Harden," he said. "Especially the infielders."

"What do I care how they play?" I asked.

"You're the shortstop, Morelli. If the other players look bad, you look bad."

There was a whistle as Coach Darby called us in for a pregame cheer. "Go back to your cage, Moochie. I gotta game to play."

"Good luck," Moochie cackled.

During the first inning, I sat next to Fish in the dugout. I couldn't stop glancing at the bleachers, hoping to see Coach Harden.

Fish popped a sunflower seed into his mouth. "Maybe he couldn't get a ticket," he said.

I grabbed a handful. "Who?"

Fish raised his hands like he was worshipping the sun. "The legendary Coach Harden," he said, his voice quaking.

"He *is* a legend," I said, watching Kenny swing and miss again.

"When he shows up, I'll ask him to sign my hat," said Fish as Kenny struck out. "Which should be just about . . . never."

"He'll be here."

Fish spun a finger by his ear. "You're delusional."

I spat out a seed. "You're jealous."

Kenny grabbed some pine next to me. "The three of us together again," he said, all smiles. "I told you it would be great."

"He's right," Fish said with a smile. "Welcome to the Pirates, you All-Star reject."

I gave him a friendly slug and settled in to watch the top of the first inning.

A few minutes later, it was our turn in the field. I jogged out to shortstop, breathing in the fresh air. I loved being on the field during a game, no matter who was there to watch. At least Dad was right in the front row, sitting with Fish's parents. He raised his fist as I left the dugout.

When I got to short, Fish was fielding a ground ball McKlusky had thrown. I looked to my left. Shane was at second base, drawing in the dirt with his toe. I hated to admit it, but Moochie was right. If these guys looked bad, so would I. I walked over to Shane.

"Yeah?" he said, wiping the dirt with his cleat. "What do you want?"

"I'll cover second on anything hit to your left," I told him. "But if it's in between us, listen for my voice. If you hear me call you off, that means I got it."

"Are you the coach now?" Shane asked.

"No, but I *am* the shortstop. That makes me like the captain of the infield."

Shane gave me a salute. "Aye-aye."

"Very funny," I said. Pretty soon, he'd be saluting me for real.

It didn't happen in the first inning, though. Caleb struck out the leadoff batter, then got the next two Dodgers to fly out.

Back in the dugout, Coach Darby read the batting order for the inning. "Julian, Roy, Luther."

Julian was up first. He struck out on three pitches. "That last one was off the plate," I said as we passed each other near the on-deck circle.

"So?" he asked, like I was bothering him.

"I'm just saying make the pitcher throw strikes. Don't swing at bad pitches."

"For your information, Roy, we already have a coach. We don't need another one."

I wasn't so sure about that, but I dropped it anyway. It was time to focus. I was up, and I was hungry for a hit. Maybe Coach Harden wasn't there, but if he started hearing stories about the new sensation in the rec league, he would have to come see it for himself.

The first pitch floated toward me like a beach ball. I swung and missed. It was *too* slow!

I didn't miss the second pitch. *Smack!* A worm burner through the shortstop's legs and into the outfield grass. I raced down the first baseline. I lifted my head. The center fielder scooped up the ball. He saw me round first base and pump-faked like he wanted to throw me out.

I inched my way toward second base. The center fielder eyed me closely.

"Throw it to the mound!" his coach yelled.

The pitcher waved his glove. "Here!"

But the center fielder couldn't resist. With a big step, he fired the ball to the first baseman. That was all I needed. I went from zero to sixty around second base.

"To the mound!" the coach yelled again.

I was dancing between third base and home now.

The pitcher was jumping up and down, waving his glove. *"Throw it here!"*

But the first baseman gunned the ball across the infield. His throw hit the dirt and rolled all the way to the fence. His teammates chased after it, but I was already safe at home.

I crossed the plate like a conquering hero. My victims were the Dodgers. And my plunder was one run. That was how I played the game.

I got a round of high fives from everyone—except Shane and Julian. They were at the other end of the bench tossing pebbles at Wyatt. Wyatt was ignoring them.

Kenny was the most excited about my inside-the-park home run. "I told you this was a good idea," he said.

Fish nodded. "We actually have a lead. For now."

Just then, Julian gestured to Fish from the other end of the dugout. "Hey, Fishman. We saved you a seat."

Fish nodded to Julian. "Catch you later," he said to me and Kenny. "I'll be down there."

"Good," I said, wondering why he was in such a hurry to hang out with the Parkside guys. "Your breath smells like old-man toe jam anyway."

"This is to remember me by then," he said, breathing into my face.

Coach Darby came up to me next. Maybe he wanted to rethink that batting order. "Good hustling, Roy." He scratched his forehead. "But be careful how you play out there. Some people might think you were showing off."

"Which people?"

"Well, the other team."

"I wasn't showing off," I told him. "I was just running the bases."

"Just be careful," Coach said. "I don't want any hurt feelings."

Feelings? What did feelings have to do with it?

I turned back to the game in time to see Luther strike out. Coach Darby clapped his hands. "Great cut, Luther! Great cut!"

After that swing, nobody was going to accuse Luther of showing off.

The game stayed close. Caleb gave up a few hits, but the Dodgers never got much going. While we were taking the field for the bottom of the seventh, I made a stop at the mound. "Three outs to go," I told Caleb. "Mow 'em down."

"Hey," he said as I was jogging away. "How come nobody makes any noise on this team? It's the last inning and you're the first person to say anything to me."

"I guess they're not used to winning," I said.

Caleb looked around at the guys. Most of them were just standing around. "I can see why."

"We're up a run. If we can hold them here, we'll win."

But nothing was that easy.

The leadoff batter popped the first pitch high into the air. I shuffled to my left, raising my glove to shield my eyes from the sun. "I got it!" I shouted, so Shane would know to back off. But just as the ball was about to fall into my glove, someone came crashing into me. I stumbled sideways. The ball hit the dirt—right between me and Shane, who was on his knees.

The runner was safe at first.

"What are you doing? I said I had it."

"It was closer to me," Shane said.

"That's not how it works. I told you. If the shortstop calls for it, the other person has to back off."

"If being the hero is so important to you, then next time I'll let you have the ball."

I walked back to short, shaking my head. I was glad Coach Harden hadn't been there to see that! He'd scratch me off his list with one stroke of his pencil. Was this team so bad that anyone who caught a ball was a hero?

Caleb blew two fastballs by the next batter. I tried to start some chatter. "Here we go!" I yelled.

"One more!" Kenny shouted from the outfield.

The batter got underneath Caleb's 0–2 pitch, lifting it high over the infield. I drifted over to back up Shane, who only had to take a step to his left to make the play.

"Your ball!" I said.

Shane went after the ball like a bored dog. When he did get under it, he held his glove to the side of his head. The ball glanced off his glove and hit the dirt. The lead runner scored and the batter was rounding second base.

"Three!" I shouted, pointing to third base.

But Shane tossed the ball to McKlusky, who was playing *first* base. The batter scored the winning run and the Dodgers went crazy, dancing on home plate.

Most of the Pirates were headed to the dugout. They didn't seem too upset about losing the game. Julian even snuck up behind McKlusky and stole his hat. They started chasing each other around the outfield.

I got in Shane's face. "You have to use two hands when you catch a pop-up," I said. "One hand inside the glove and one hand behind it."

Shane glared back. "I know how to play baseball."

"Then why didn't you catch the ball?"

Shane looked over at Fish, who had been standing a few feet away, listening. "Fishman, tell your friend to chill. Doesn't he know its just a game?"

Fish opened his mouth, but I cut him off.

"It's a game we just lost. Because of you."

"*You're* the new guy, All-Star. Not me. If you don't like the way we play, go find another team." Then he turned and jogged off the field.

"What's with him?" I asked Fish, thinking that if I could find another team, I wouldn't be on this one.

"He's cool," said Fish. "And I'll tell him you are too. But you gotta remember this isn't the All-Star League. Things are a little different for us."

I wondered what Coach Darby would have to say about the game. Even a softie like him would have to let Shane hear it for not hustling.

"Fellas," he said. "You all played a great game today." He cruised around the circle giving us high fives. "Did everyone have fun?"

"I did," said McKlusky.

"Me too," Kenny added.

A chill went down my spine. If this is what the Pirates thought was fun, I was in for a long season.

· 12 ·

It rained all day Sunday and Monday. At times, there weren't even drops, just a thin mist that soaked everything slowly, like someone was wandering around Pilchuck with a spray bottle. After school on Monday, I made my way to the Pilchuck library, feeling as gloomy as the weather.

The rain picked up as I walked the last few blocks, and the water seeped through my shoes. I sloshed my way to a back room, where the tutoring group was supposed to meet.

I poked my head inside and turned to stone when I saw who was there.

Valerie.

"You?" she said. "What are you doing here?"

"I'm here for tutoring," I told her. "Why are you

here? Is this where the girls who are too good for everyone meet?"

"Not everyone," she said. "Just you." She gave me a suspicious look. "Did you plan this?"

"Uh, no," I said. "Why?"

"Because it's all your fault I'm here. If you hadn't gotten me in trouble with Mr. Downer—again."

"Again?"

"He called my house on Friday. And now my parents are making me join this lame tutoring group." Valerie looked around the room. "Where is everyone else?"

There was a knock on the door.

"Thank you," Valerie said to the ceiling as Camille walked into the room.

Even though I had only met her once, it was weird seeing her now. Kind of like running into a teacher out of school, only *this* teacher was dating my dad. "Hello, everyone," she said. "Well, both of you."

"Hi," I said back.

She smiled. "Good to see you again, Roy." Then she offered her hand to Valerie.

"Again?" Valerie said to me. "Have you been here before?"

"She teaches at my sister's school," I said, thinking quickly.

Camille gave me a quick look but didn't say anything. Instead, she turned the other way. "You must be

Valerie. It's nice to meet you. I'm Camille—and I'll be your history tutor."

I wish that's all you were, I thought. I sat down, cursing my luck. Of all the women in the world, what did I do to get stuck in a room with these two?

"So," Camille said, joining us at the round table. "Do you two know each other?"

"We're in the same history class," Valerie told Camille. "Let me fill you in. Roy doesn't like me because I don't like him. And I don't like Roy because I have standards."

"I have no standards," I said, crossing my arms. "That's why I liked her."

"Very clever," said Valerie. "But FYI, I'm out of *your* league, not the other way around."

"Fine with me. I like my league."

Valerie turned to Camille. "In his league, they dress like the whole day is gym class and they throw trash at innocent people."

"We're low maintenance," I said. "So what?"

"More like no maintenance," said Valerie.

Camille put her hands on the table. "Okay, okay," she said. "We only have an hour, so let's get to work. Why don't you each tell me about your history class."

"Pointless," said Valerie. "Every day is the same. We read a chapter for homework. But in class the next day, we read the same chapter out loud."

Camille looked at me. "Roy?"

"You want to know what I think about history?"

"Please," said Camille. "And be honest."

I made two thumbs-up, then flipped my fists upside down and made a sound like air going out of a tire. "That's what I think of history."

Valerie looked at Camille. "You see what I'm talking about?"

"What *exactly* don't you like about history?" Camille asked. "Without the sound effects."

"You told me to be honest," I said.

"What don't you like, Roy?" she repeated.

I pulled out my textbook and let it fall open on the table. "*That's* what I don't like about history," I said, waving at the pages of text. "It's just names and dates and it goes on and on for like three thousand years. How am I supposed to memorize all that?"

"Why would we even want to?" Valerie added. "It has nothing to do with us."

Camille closed the book and took it off the table. "Before we go any further," she said, "I want you both to know that I'm not here to sell you anything. I'm here to help you get through the school year. So let's make a deal. I won't talk about how much I love history, and you won't talk about how much you hate it. But you will keep an open mind and do what I say without debate. Okay?"

"Fine with me," said Valerie.

"Roy—do we have a deal?"

"Fine," I said. "It's a deal."

Camille smiled. "Next question. What are you studying in class right now?"

"We're studying slavery," Valerie told Camille. "And Mexico and something about states."

"Anything else?" Camille asked. She looked at me for an answer. "Roy?"

"Hey, you're the expert," I said.

Camille was quiet for a minute. I wondered if she was going to kick me out of the room. But where could she send me? I knew she couldn't make me go to the principal's office. Then she said calmly, "You should both know that your parents have asked me to keep them up to date about your progress in these sessions. They also said that if I have any trouble, I shouldn't hesitate to talk to them about you."

That one hit me like a brick. It was bad enough that Camille was my tutor. But having her call home? Ugly. Which parent would she call? Dad? Or worse . . . Mom?

Camille went on. "I don't know about you guys, but the less your parents have to be involved, the easier it would be for me. Would you agree?"

"Definitely," Valerie said.

Camille looked at me and I nodded quickly. That was one thing Valerie and I saw eye to eye on.

Camille glanced up at the clock. "Here's how I want to do this. Since you two seem to be good at drama, I'm going to give you an assignment that involves some acting." She looked at me first. "Roy, your name is Dred Scott." She looked at Valerie. "Your name is Irene Sanford Emerson. Do those names sound familiar?"

"Dred Scott does," Valerie said.

"It rings a bell," I lied.

Camille explained the assignment. "Your job is to do some research and come back next Monday ready to talk about yourselves."

"That's it?" Valerie asked. "Just talk about myself?"

"She won't need tutoring for that," I muttered.

Before we left, Camille handed us each a piece of paper. "What's this?" Valerie asked.

Camille tapped Valerie's sheet and beamed. "Five keys to making your history problems history."

Valerie read her sheet. "'Sit in the front row. Read one hour every night. Take notes. Don't memorize. Give yourself a chance.'" She looked up. "That doesn't sound too hard."

"What do you think, Roy?" Camille asked.

All I knew was that I didn't see how these five things were supposed to help me in history. "Can't you just tell us what we need to know and what stuff we can ignore?"

Camille shook her head. "There are no shortcuts, Roy. But if you put in the time, you'll do great, I swear."

"Easy for you to say," I grumbled, stuffing the piece of paper in my pocket.

The rain had stopped by the time I left the library. *Wonderful*, I thought. *Now I can stare out my window at the sun while I figure out who Dred Scott is.* I only made it worse by taking the long way home past Boardman Park. I thought it would cheer me up, but that was before I ran into Ruben, Derek, and Moochie.

Ruben and Derek were wearing their All-Star warm-up pants. Moochie had a blue and gold batting glove on each hand.

"I guess you're going to practice," I said as we stood near the drinking fountains outside the grandstand.

"Every day at five," said Derek.

Did he have to remind me it was every day?

"That's not all," said Moochie. "After practice we're going to the high school game. Coach Harden is giving us a personal tour of the stadium."

"It should be fun," said Ruben. "We're going to meet the whole team."

"Since we're going to be playing with most of them next year," Moochie added, with an evil twinkle in his eye.

"Too bad you can't be there," said Derek.

I could be there if one of you jerks invites me, I thought. Not that I expected Moochie to do that. But Ruben and Derek were supposed to be my friends. It got awkward when nobody spoke up, so after a moment I said, "I can't make it. I gotta do this thing and it's pretty important."

In the background a whistle blew. Ruben looked over his shoulder. "We better get going," he said. "Don't want to keep Coach Burke waiting—right, Mooch?"

So that's how it is, I thought as they jogged toward the grandstand. They were getting a private tour of the high school stadium, and I was going home to read about Dred Scott. Whoever that was.

· 13 ·

Mom found Camille's list that night. Like an idiot, I had left it in the back pocket of my pants and thrown them in the laundry. Rookie mistake.

So every night that week, she followed me to my room and called out the time. "Eight o'clock," she said on Monday. "I don't want to hear that door open for one hour."

"Fine," I said.

"I'll be standing right here," she said, pointing to a spot on the floor.

"Your choice," I said, going into my room.

"Take notes," she said through the closed door. "And give yourself a chance."

I did stay in my room for the full hour every night. But I didn't read much history. I couldn't bring myself to turn the page of a chapter about something called "Whigs and the Compromise of 1850." Instead, I spent more time on my other classes. On Friday, we were going to have a quiz in earth science, and even though I was all caught up on the reading for that class, I decided to reread a couple of chapters. It was better than reading about Whigs.

By Friday, I was feeling pretty good about my chances on the science quiz. Still, when Ruben told me about his guaranteed system for acing multiple-choice tests, I had to listen.

Just before class began he leaned over and whispered, "Unless you know the answer for sure, you never guess the highest or lowest number. And if there's an answer like *both A and B,* that's usually the money. Otherwise, why would they bother putting it in there?"

"Thanks," I said, wishing Ruben had told me this *before* I had to quit the All-Star team.

"Oh, and one more thing," he whispered. "It's never, *ever* the same letter twice in a row."

"Got it," I said, just as Mr. Packer put my science quiz in front of me.

There were twenty questions on the quiz, and I knew most of them right away. When I had to guess, I followed Ruben's advice, but I didn't need it as much as I thought I would. I'd find out for sure next week, when we got the quizzes back.

* * *

On Saturday, Dad drove me to Boardman Park. Mom was with Sara, who was taking her driver's test. She'd probably ace that test too. I was glad there had been no sign of Camille. I didn't want to answer any questions about Dred Scott before I figured out who he was, which I would tomorrow. For now, I needed to focus on baseball.

The real action that day started in the third inning. The Angels had a runner on second base, when their catcher hit a line drive to center field.

I stood on the edge of the infield, waving my glove. I was the cutoff man, and Julian was supposed to throw it to me so we could hold the runner at third base.

But Julian tossed the ball into the middle of the infield, where there was nobody to catch it. That let the runner score.

After the inning, I waited for Julian as he came in from the outfield. "If I'm waving my glove like that, it means I'm the cutoff man. If you have the ball, throw it to me."

"Thanks for the advice," Julian said. "I'll be sure to remember that."

"It's not advice. It's the way you play baseball."

"No," said Luther. "It's the way *you* play baseball. We play the way we like."

"Can you back me up here?" I asked Fish.

"Hey, don't look at me," he said, going with Luther and Julian. "I told you this wasn't the All-Star team."

What was that about? Doesn't anyone on this team care about the way we play?

The trouble on the field continued in the fifth, with the score tied at four. The shortstop led off with a slow roller up the third baseline. Fish set his feet and got the ball out of his glove with plenty of time. But his throw was too slow and the runner was safe at first.

"Don't be afraid to charge those," I said.

Fish kicked the dirt. "Stop telling people what to do, Roy. Seriously."

During the next at bat, I watched the runner. Every time Caleb pitched, he jumped off the base like he couldn't wait to get moving.

I bent my knees and rocked on my feet as Caleb started his windup. The batter swung. *BAM!* A bullet right back to the mound! The runner took off. Caleb snared the ball and stared at his glove as the crowd cheered.

The runner skidded to a stop and scooted back to first.

"Way to go, Caleb!" Coach Darby shouted.

Now there was one out. We could still get out of the inning with a double play. But the next batter ripped a ball right to third base that bounced off Fish's glove. Fish reached down, but it took him two tries to get a grip on the ball. He rifled a bad throw over Julian's head. Now there were runners on second and third.

Caleb slapped his hand against his glove in

frustration. Fish turned red. He stared at his feet. I knew why he was upset. Because of him, there were two runners in scoring position, with one out.

"Better to hold on to that," I told him.

"Don't tell me how to play," Fish shot back.

Then do it right, I wanted to tell him.

Next up was a guy who looked like he was big enough to swing a cedar tree. I pounded my fist against the inside of my glove and watched him strut to the plate like he was the new Babe Ruth.

More like my aunt Ruth.

The batter scanned the infield, looking for a hole. I spit on my right hand. Enough was enough. I was going to get Fish off the hook and get Caleb out of the inning.

I took a step in. Out of the corner of my eye, I could see the runner on third take a long lead toward home. If I was playing in close, I might have enough time to hold him on base or tag him out.

The batter dug in, then slid his front foot away from the plate. A smile crept across my face. He had just shown me exactly where he wanted to hit the ball.

Staying in a crouch, I sidestepped toward third base. On the mound, Caleb delivered a fastball, inside. The batter swung, sending a hard-hit grounder toward third, just like I thought.

I charged past Fish and got the ball in my glove, then set my feet and whipped my arm forward. But I didn't throw it. Behind me, the runner broke for home. He had no idea I still had the ball. The pump fake had worked! I reached out, tagged him, then fired a real throw to first to get Aunt Ruth out by half a step.

Double play. Inning over.

"Nice play," said Caleb as I hustled past the mound. "You had me fooled."

"Just doing my thing," I said, looking out for Fish.

But Fish wasn't happy. "Why'd you cut me off?" he asked when we were in the dugout. "I *had* that."

"Who cares who made the play? We're out of the inning."

"That was my ball," he said angrily.

"What'd you expect?" Shane asked. "You're playing next to an All-Star. You should be bowing at his feet."

"And kissing his shoes," Julian added.

"Say that again," I said to Julian, "and your lips won't be the only thing these shoes touch."

That was when Coach Darby jumped in. "Okay, okay," he said. "Settle down. We're all here to have fun."

"Tell that to Roy," Julian said as Coach Darby pulled me out of the dugout. "He's too busy being a superstar."

"It's not as easy as it looks, chump," I said.

"That's *enough*, Roy," said Coach. "You have to remember, this is not the All-Star League. In this league, we don't go out of our way to show up the other players."

"I wasn't showing up anyone. The guy left the bag. I tagged him fair and square."

Coach Darby shook his head. "There are the rules of the game, and then there are the rules of good sportsmanship. It's possible to follow one without following the other. Think about that."

I did think about it. But I also thought about what Dad had told me—that there was no rule against playing my best.

I watched Coach Darby walk over to the dugout and call out the batting order for the sixth inning. "Shane, Kenny, Julian," he said.

I took a seat on the end of the bench. Fish sat with the Parkside guys. Kenny sat with McKlusky, Wyatt, and Caleb. It was the bottom of the seventh inning when Caleb finally joined me.

"I thought it was a good play earlier," he told me.

"Me too," said Wyatt, coming toward us.

"You guys don't think I was showing off?" I asked.

"No way," Caleb said. "You're just trying to make a play." He pointed at Fish, Julian, Shane, and Luther, who were at the other end of the dugout. "They don't like it because it makes them look lazy."

We ended up losing the game 7–4. After the final out, Coach delivered another pep talk. "Good work out there, everyone," he said. "Wyatt, way to keep your eye on the ball. McKlusky, you're doing a great job keeping your foot on first base."

"This guy sure is easy to please," Caleb whispered. "He might pass out when we win a game."

"*If* we win," I said, relieved that someone saw things the way I did.

Coach looked at me and Caleb. "Is there something you want to say?" he asked.

Actually, I did. "All that stuff is great," I said. "But I was thinking there are some fielding drills we could do to get even better."

"Well," said Coach, "that's up to the group. I want to make sure everyone is having fun. Winning doesn't matter as much as that."

"I can tell you my answer right now," Julian said. "That would be *N–O*."

"Same here," Luther said.

"*N–O* for me too," Shane said. "Drills are like homework. We just want to hit. Isn't that right, Wyatt?"

Wyatt shrugged. "I guess so, yeah," he said meekly.

"Four to one," Shane said.

"How do the rest of you feel?" Coach asked.

Caleb's hand shot up. "Count me in," he said.

McKlusky spoke up next. "I like having fun. But I like winning too. I think I'm with Roy."

"Four to *three*," I said, staring at Shane. Then I looked at Kenny and Fish. "Anyone *else* with me?"

Kenny raised his hand slowly, but stopped halfway when Fish shot him a look. "I guess I just want to have fun," he said.

Shane pumped his fist. "Five to three! No drills!" He high-fived Julian, Luther, and Fish.

"I guess he does like to win," Caleb muttered to me.

"Yeah," I said. "Just not baseball."

Fish had the final vote. It wouldn't change anything, but we all looked at him, wondering what he was going to say. "I like things the way they are," he announced at last. "I think we should just have fun too."

"Six to three!" Shane cheered again. "What a rout!"

I dug my foot in the dirt and glared sideways at Fish. I knew he was annoyed about that ground ball, but I had still hoped he would back me up. After all, I'd been his friend a lot longer than Julian and Shane.

Coach called for everyone to settle down before he dismissed us. When practice was over, I walked up to Fish. "Why are you being like this?" I asked.

"What do you mean?"

"Why are you taking their side?"

"Don't look at me," said Fish. "It's because of you that I had to take sides in the first place."

· 14 ·

Mom and Sara met me and Dad in the parking lot after the game. I was already in the truck. Light rain was falling. All I wanted to do was get away from Boardman Park as quickly as possible.

Sara ran up to Dad, waving a small plastic card. "I passed the test. I got my driver's license!" She held out her hand. "Keys, please?"

Great, I thought. *She doesn't even have to go to school to pass a test.*

Dad looked at Mom. "Is it okay?" he asked.

Mom shrugged. "Fine with me."

Dad hugged Sara and handed her the keys. Sara hopped into the driver's side of the truck.

Mom walked over to the passenger window. "How

was the game?" she asked, pulling up the hood of her raincoat.

"We lost. The team is terrible. There's nothing I can do about it. End of story."

Dad stuck his hands in his pockets and faced Mom. "How're things?"

"Busy," she said. "School is tough."

"I think it's great you're doing that, Tee," Dad said. "I told Roy the other day how I wish I could do it over again. I didn't take school very seriously the first time."

"Maybe that's why you're going out with a teacher," I said.

Dad blushed and Mom looked back at her car. "I should go," she said quickly. She gave me a quick kiss through the window of the truck, then pulled back and looked me in the eye. "Do I have to say it?" she asked.

"No," I said. "I'll do my homework."

Mom glanced at Dad. "Really, Mike. He needs to get his homework done before Sunday afternoon. I don't want him waiting until the last minute."

"I promise," Dad said, climbing in next to me. I scooted to the middle of the seat. Sara started up the engine. Dad waved both hands. "Clutch!" he hollered. Suddenly the truck jumped forward, then died. Sara was behind the wheel, laughing.

"Have fun," Mom said. "Wear your seat belt."

Raindrops were splashing against the windshield as

Sara eased the truck away from Boardman Park. "Good," said Dad. "Now let out the clutch and press the accelerator." The truck slowed and began to shimmy. "Other pedal, Sara. The middle one." This time, the truck rolled forward.

"Looks like you got off the field just in time," he said, reaching over to turn on the windshield wipers.

"Maybe I never should have been *on* the field," I said.

"Did something happen today?" he asked. "I saw your coach pull you aside. What did he tell you?"

"Not to show up the other players," I said. "Which I didn't do. All I did was tag out a runner and throw out a batter. How is that showing them up?" I looked at the speedometer as Sara turned on to Verlot Street. We were going six miles per hour.

"Maybe he wasn't talking about the other team, pal."

"Who else is there?" I asked, replaying the moment in my mind. The runner leading off. Me charging past Fish for the ground ball. Wait. He couldn't mean . . . "You think I showed up *Fish*?"

Sara sped up to ten miles per hour. The truck groaned. "You need to shift gears," Dad told her. "Clutch in, stick down." Then to me, he added, "I'm not saying you did. I'm only saying I could imagine how it felt from Fish's point of view."

"What about mine? Are you *ever* going to see things

my way?" I asked. I was getting a little tired of Dad seeing it everyone else's way.

"Roy, I'm not taking sides here. And as far as school goes, the only side anyone in this family is on is yours. But I can imagine how it might have looked to Fish when you ran in front of him to field that ball."

"Well, you were the one who told me to play my best. So I was just doing what you told me to do."

"And I'm not changing my story," Dad said. "You should play your best. But you have to trust your teammates too. Otherwise they're going to resent you."

"Resent me?"

"They're going to wish you weren't around."

"But they need me."

"No more or less than you need them, Roy."

What did I need them for? *I* was the prospect. The only person I needed this season was Coach Harden.

Sara eased the truck up to the curb. We were in front of Dad's building now.

"Let's park around back," said Dad.

Sara held on to the wheel with both hands. The truck was still running. "Can I go to Izzy's?" she asked sweetly. "I promised her I'd come over when I got my license. I'll drive straight there and come right back."

"Maybe later," he said. "Izzy gets to see you all week. I only get every other weekend."

"You don't have to worry about me, Dad," Sara said. "I got a perfect score on my test."

"I'm not worried about you," said Dad, winking at Sara. "I'm worried about my truck."

"So what *are* we going to do tonight?" Sara asked, unclicking her seat belt.

"Ball game's on," I told Dad.

Dad scratched his chin and looked away, like he was getting ready to deliver bad news. "I kind of invited someone over to dinner."

"Wait a second," I said as we walked up the stairs to Dad's apartment. "Camille is coming for dinner? *Tonight?*" I couldn't believe Dad would do this to me.

Dad unlocked the door. "I hope that's okay."

I kicked off my shoes. One of them slammed against the closet door. How could Dad think it was okay? I had been looking forward to watching the game. Now I'd have to sit across the table from my stupid tutor, who was going to quiz me about Dred Scott.

Sara leaned against the counter and frowned. "So I don't get to see my friends, but you get to see yours?"

"I'll make you a deal," Dad said, inspecting the kitchen. "You can drive to Izzy's tomorrow, if you help me clean right now."

Sara picked up a rag, then came into the living room. "Look at me," she said. "I'm cleaning the house for Dad's girlfriend. I feel like Cinderella."

"That's funny," I said. "Because you look like the horse she took to the ball."

I had to admit one thing, though. Seeing Sara in a bad mood made me feel just a little bit better.

I avoided Camille for as long as I could. I washed my hands twice and made up a story about having to change my socks. But once dinner was served, there was nowhere to hide. With plates and glasses for four people, plus two candlesticks and a vase of flowers, there wasn't much space—on the table or around it. I had to sit with my legs folded in and my arms pinned up against my sides.

For a while, the only sounds were forks clacking against plates. Then Dad crossed his arms and pointed to Camille and me. "So I guess you two will be seeing each other Monday."

Camille smiled. "Back to work. Right, Dred?"

I wanted to vanish.

"Who's Dred?" Dad asked.

"I think she means Dred Scott, Dad," Sara said. "He was a slave." Then, like the nerd she was, Sara had to give us the guy's whole life story. I heard the words *Missouri* and *Supreme Court*, then tuned out until she was done.

"Wow," Dad said with a laugh. "I guess I haven't gotten to that chapter in the book yet. So do you and Camille see each other at school?"

Sara shook her head. "She teaches twelfth graders, Dad. I'm in tenth grade."

"Oh," Dad said.

"I've heard your name, though," Camille told Sara. "You played Eliza in the spring play last year, right? In *My Fair Lady.*"

Sara nearly choked on her food. "That was Sara *Barber,*" she said, horrified. "We look *nothing* like each other."

"You mean she can look in a mirror without breaking it?" I asked.

Sara kicked me under the table.

"I'm so sorry," said Camille. "It must be hard enough having a teacher from your school here. And then I go and confuse you with someone else . . ."

"Don't be silly," said Dad. "It was an honest mistake." He placed his big hand on top of Camille's, patted it twice, then squeezed.

Now I was about to choke. Dad holding hands with Camille was worse than people at school holding hands in the hallway. It was just painful and embarrassing for everyone. Especially while we were eating. Couldn't they wait until they were sharing a bucket of popcorn at the movies? It was too much to take. "I gotta go to the bathroom," I said to Dad. "I'll be back."

I closed the bathroom door behind me and wished there was a window I could climb out. There were so many things I would rather do than watch Dad act like a dope around Camille. Like remove my teeth with a spoon or go camping with Mr. Downer. The old goober had held me after class on Thursday to remind me that we had a test next week.

Now hearing Camille's voice from the dining room just made me more mad.

When I got back to the table, Camille and my dad were talking about history. "I told Roy about the book you gave me," he said.

"It was nothing," Camille told me.

"Nothing?" Dad replied. "It's fascinating. Roy, did you know when Columbus and his sailors came ashore in the New World, the Indians brought them parrots?"

"It's better than what Columbus brought the Indians," Sara said. "Unless you'd rather have smallpox than a bird."

"Huh," said Dad, sounding a little embarrassed. "I guess I'm the only one who didn't know that."

"Maybe *you* should get a tutor," I said.

"I'm not sure it would help," Dad said with a nervous laugh. He gave me the *watch it* look, then stood up and patted his stomach. "I think I'll get started on the dishes."

Camille got ready to leave. "Thanks for dinner," she said to all of us. "Sara, I'll see you around school. And, Roy, I guess I'll see you tomorrow."

"Can't wait," I said, watching Dad follow Camille out to her car.

I watched TV while Sara talked quietly on her phone. "No," she was saying. "It was totally weird. Iz, she thought I was Sara *Barber*. . . . I know! That's what I said. Yeah, if your parents ever get divorced, do not let one of them bring home a teacher from your school. . . ."

I woke up the next morning to the scent of pancakes and bacon. *Now,* this *is what weekends at Dad's are all about,* I thought as I made my way to the dining room—big breakfasts, lazy mornings, maybe a game of catch in the park if the sun was shining.

"Blueberries or plain?" Dad asked. He was standing over the stove holding a spatula. A bowl of batter sat nearby on the counter.

"Blueberry," I said, sitting down at the table.

"Plain," Sara said, from the other side of the table. She flipped her phone open, glanced at it, then quickly closed it. "I can drive to Izzy's today, right?"

"That was the deal," Dad said, carrying over a stack of pancakes.

"What are we doing?" I asked.

Dad put a hand on my shoulder. "*You* are going to learn everything you can about Dred Scott," he said. "I promised your mom you'd get it done before you went back to her place."

"All right," I grumbled, knowing I had put it off as long as I could.

"And just so there are no distractions, I'm going to go with your sister."

"Excuse me?" she choked. "Did you say you were going *with* me?"

"I'll wait in the truck," he said. "That's the deal. Take it or leave it."

Sara filled a glass with juice. "Fine," she muttered. "I'll take it."

After breakfast, Dad and Sara left and I was alone in the apartment. Even though nobody else was around, I knew I was cornered. I needed to do my assignment for Camille. I'd heard Sara tell Dad at dinner last night that Dred Scott was a slave. That was a start. But if I didn't show up at the library with more information than that, I'd be a dead man.

I pulled a chair up to the computer in the den and got on the Internet. I had to warm up, though, so instead of searching for Dred Scott, I searched for Roy Morelli. Maybe there were stories about the best baseball player in Pilchuck. But there wasn't anything about me yet—just an article about someone named Roy Morelli who'd won a rodeo in Wyoming. That sounded a lot cooler than what I was doing, so I kept looking. I was still reading about all the Roy Morellis in the world when the door opened. I looked at the time. I'd been online for an hour and a half. Dad and Sara were here, and any minute, Mom would be too!

"I'll be in my room," Sara said. "Tell me when Mom gets here."

Dad walked up to me. "Looks like you've been busy," he said. "What did you find out?"

I was really in a jam here. I had to come up with *something* relevant about Dred Scott. What had Sara said at dinner? I remembered Missouri and the Supreme Court. Maybe that was enough. "Well, um, Dred Scott was from Missouri and he was a slave who went to the Supreme Court, which is next to the White House, where the president lives." I pointed to the screen. "There's a lot more here, so I think I'm done."

"I don't think the Supreme Court is next to the White House," Dad said, looking unconvinced. He squinted over my shoulder at the screen. "Who's Roy Morelli from Jersey City?"

"Oh, that?" I said, closing the screen. "That's, um, extra credit."

"What else did you learn for tomorrow?"

"You know, the Civil War and Abraham Lincoln. It all goes together." I looked Dad in the eye. "Trust me."

"I trust you," he said. "But promise me if you have any questions, you'll ask Camille. I know you have a test this week."

"I promise," I said, wishing I could go five minutes without someone reminding me about my next exam.

· 15 ·

"So," said Camille Monday afternoon. "Dred and Irene. Who wants to go first?"

"I will," said Valerie.

Camille smiled. "Great! Why don't you tell me about yourself, Irene?"

Valerie sat up straight and folded her hands on the table. "My name is Irene Sanford Emerson," she said. "And I lived in the 1800s. I'm dead now." She flipped her hair back. "Obviously."

Camille nodded. "Where did you live, Irene?"

"A lot of places," Valerie said. "But mostly in Missouri."

"Were you married?"

"My husband was a doctor in the army. We moved around a lot."

I sank in my seat. Valerie knew way more about her person than I knew about mine. Talk about showing someone up!

"Who is *we*?" Camille asked.

"Our family. And our slaves." Valerie paused. "That sounds weird to say."

"It wasn't weird to Irene," Camille said.

"Well, one of them was named Dred Scott, and he wanted to be freed, but I wouldn't do it."

Camille smiled. "You did great, Irene." She looked at me. "Can we hear from Dred Scott now?"

"That's me," I said. "Dred Scott."

"What's your story, Dred?" Camille asked.

"Um, I was a guy. I lived a long time ago. I died."

Camille gestured for me to keep talking. "Where did you live?"

"In America?"

"Time out," said Camille. "Roy, I gave you an assignment. You were supposed to find out who Dred Scott was. Now tell me one fact about yourself or go out there and look one up."

"Okay," I said. "He was a slave. I mean, I was a slave. I had to do whatever anyone told me to do. Life sucked. I died."

Camille snapped her fingers three times. "Work with me, Dred. Tell me what you did about your situation."

"I can't remember. I'm sorry. I'm not good at this."

"Roy, stop trying to remember facts and just imagine you are Dred Scott. How would you feel if you were him?"

"I don't know how I would feel. All I know is I was a slave and I didn't want to be one."

"Good," said Camille. "You're a slave and you would rather be free. What would you do?"

"I'd run away," I said.

"Is that what you did?"

"I guess so."

"Is that what happened, Irene?" Camille asked.

Valerie came at me guns blazing. "You didn't run away, you dumb slave. You tried to buy your freedom, *from me*. Because I owned you. And I wouldn't let you. So we went to court. And you *lost*."

"That's garbage. I should have been free."

"Why?" asked Camille.

"Because I lived in Missouri," I replied, remembering more of what Sara had said the other night. "And that was a free state. But this overlord kept me anyway because she's greedy and heartless."

"Hey," said Valerie. "I was just following the law. You were my property. There's nothing greedy about a person wanting to keep her own property. How else was I supposed to make money?"

"Ever hear of a *job*?" I asked.

"Remember, this is the 1850s," Camille said. "There weren't a lot of ways for a woman to make a living."

"How am I supposed to know that?" I asked, wishing she would stop looking down on me just because I didn't love history like everyone else did. "I'm just a slave."

"You're pretending to be a slave," said Camille. "But as Roy, you should know that women—"

"Well, I don't," I said. "I already told you. I'm not good at this."

"I think you are," said Camille.

"Well, sorry to disappoint you. But I'm not."

"Not good at this," Camille said, "or not trying?"

I looked across the table and made eye contact with Valerie. For the first time around her, I felt very small. Even more than I did that day at the market. "I am trying," I said. "I'm here, aren't I?"

"You're here," Camille replied. "But that's about all." Her light blue eyes were locked on mine. "You want to know what I think?"

"What?"

"I think you're afraid that if you do try, you'll do well. And if you do well, everyone will expect you to do it again."

The longer this conversation went on, the more uncomfortable I got. I shifted in my seat. "Hey, it's not my problem our teacher doesn't teach us anything," I said.

"Is it his fault you're throwing trash around the room?" Valerie asked.

"You're free to go, Valerie," Camille said politely. "I'm just going to finish this conversation with Roy."

Looking sheepish, Valerie pulled her things together and slipped out of the room.

Camille turned back to me. "You have a teacher who doesn't motivate you. I get that. But is that really a reason to tank the class? Your parents have high expectations, Roy. You don't have to lower them to meet them."

Neither of us said anything. Camille looked at me and I looked at the clock.

"Can I go now?" I asked after thirty long seconds had passed.

Camille nodded. "You're dismissed," she said quietly.

I left the room as quickly as I could. I just wanted to get away from the library. But Valerie was waiting for me outside the front door. I hurried past her, but she was on my heels.

"Wait up," she said as we passed through a set of double doors and into the main room of the library.

"What?" I asked.

"What's with you?" she asked.

"What do you mean?"

"I mean, what's with the 'I can't do it' routine?" she said, walking quickly to keep up.

"What do you care?"

"I have to sit in a room and listen to you," she said. "I can't believe I'm saying this, but it actually makes me miss the old Roy."

• 16 •

On Tuesday, I brought home some good news—a B+ on my science quiz! "I'm so proud of you," Mom gushed that night as she stuck my paper to the refrigerator, covering half of Sara's latest English paper. "See what happens when you put in the effort?"

"I got lucky," I said, trying to keep Mom from being *too* enthusiastic. I didn't want her expecting this kind of thing every day.

"Is that really what happened?" she asked.

"No," I said, joking around. "I'm actually a world-famous scientist and the water cycle happens to be my expertise."

Secretly, though, Mom was probably right. I *had* put in the effort. But I also had Ruben's advice to fall back on.

It was just in time too, because my history test was in three days. Suddenly, I was oozing with confidence. I could feel the difference. Roy Morelli was a multiple-choice-test-taking machine. And if there *was* a question I didn't know, all I had to do was remember Ruben's rules and I'd be home free.

Mom looked more stressed than usual Thursday night. "I have to go to the library," she said. "There's a book I need for a paper I'm supposed to finish tonight."

"I can drive you there," Sara said.

Mom shook her head. "No, I need you to stay here and help Roy. He has a test tomorrow and I want you to make sure he's ready."

Sara shrugged. "Sounds like teaching a dog to do algebra, but I'll do my best."

"Thank you, sweetie," Mom said as she hurried out the door.

"Are you ready for your test?" Sara asked.

"Absolutely," I said. "I got a system."

Sara's eyes narrowed. "You're not cheating, are you?"

"No way. It's totally legit."

"Good," Sara said. "Because I have better things to do than babysit you."

The room was unusually quiet when I walked in to history class the next day and took my seat. Valerie turned around to face me. "Are you nervous?"

"No way. I'm gonna blow this test up." I spread my hands apart and made a sound like an explosion.

Valerie looked surprised. "Have you been studying?"

"Let's just say I'm ready for action."

"Oh-*kay*," Valerie said. "Well, good luck."

Luck has nothing to do with it, I thought as Mr. Downer passed out the tests. I dove right in and read the first question, a pencil in my hand.

> **In the case of *Marbury v. Madison,* in 1803, the Supreme Court established the principle of:**
>
> **(a) habeas corpus**
> **(b) the right to privacy**
> **(c) judicial review**
> **(d) both (a) and (b)**

Cha-ching! I thought. I didn't know the answer for sure, but I remembered what Ruben had said about answers like "d." So I checked that one and moved on.

> **On which date did South Carolina secede from the Union?**
>
> **(a) December 20, 1860**
> **(b) March 6, 1857**
> **(c) December 29, 1845**
> **(d) none of the above**

I had to guess that one too. Luckily, I knew it was *b* because it was never the highest or lowest numbers.

As the test went on, I was more and more thankful that I had a system because I didn't know as many answers as I had on the earth science quiz. So maybe I wouldn't go home with a B+ again, I thought, putting my pencil down. But I was pretty sure I had done well enough to get a B.

· 17 ·

As I laced up my cleats before our game against the
Reds that weekend, I peeked at the bleachers. I
saw Mom and Sara in the front row. Dad was talking to
Fish's parents in the second row. And there, on the top
row, holding a notebook and chewing on the end of a
pencil, was Coach Harden.

I felt like I'd been hit by a bolt of lightning. This is
how it was supposed to happen! In the swing of a bat
and the flash of a glove, all his questions would be answered. Could I hit? Yes! Could I field? Yes! Could I
run? Yes!

There was still a little time before the first pitch, so
I decided to ask Fish if he wanted to throw the ball
around. I found him standing alone just outside the
dugout.

"Hey, Fish," I said, holding out a ball. "How about it?"

"I don't think so, man. I'm gonna go warm up with those guys." He pointed to Julian and Shane.

"Come on," I said. "I promise I won't throw too hard."

Fish shook his head. "Unbelievable." Then he turned his back and jogged across the field to where Shane and Julian were waiting.

"I'll throw with you," Caleb said, appearing at my side. "If you want."

"Sure," I said, disappointed to see that Fish wasn't paying attention. "Let's do it."

My big chance to finally impress Coach Harden came in the third inning. Caleb was on first base and McKlusky was on second. There was one out. Fish was batting ahead of me. In the first inning, he'd struck out, and I could tell he was off his game. But by then, I noticed something in the field that could help him. So I stopped him as he walked to the plate.

"What now?" he asked.

"The third baseman is playing back," I said.

"So?"

"It might be a good time to lay one down."

"You want me to bunt?" he asked.

"The way the third baseman's playing, you'll probably get on. Even if you don't, you'll move the runners up—and stay out of the double play."

Fish looked disgusted. "You think I can't get a hit,"

he said. "You're worried I'll end the inning and you won't get to knock in a couple of runners in front of Coach Harden."

Fish was right, in a way. I was afraid he'd ground out. But I was trying to help him for the sake of the team, not just for myself.

The ump interrupted us. "Batter up!" he said.

"It's just smart baseball, Fish."

He grabbed a bat. "You want a bunt so bad, you bunt."

"Why would *I* bunt?"

"Oh, that's right," said Fish. "The superstar is too good to bunt. He just tells everyone else when to do it." Then he turned his back and walked to the plate.

On the first pitch, Fish proved me wrong. He slapped a single through the gap between first base and second base, getting on and advancing the runners.

That meant the bases were loaded, and I was up. I looked at the pitcher, daring him to give me something over the plate.

A moment later, the pitcher threw me an outside pitch that hung like a balloon. I opened my stance and swung at the ball like I never wanted to see it again. A home run!

I could hear the ooohs from the crowd as I rounded the bases. Not everyone was impressed. "Lucky," the second baseman said. "Enjoy it," the third baseman added. I kept going, imagining the celebration waiting for me at home plate. Even *this* team couldn't ignore a hit like that, could they? I imagined a mob of guys pounding me on the helmet and slapping me on the back. Then, from the home stretch, I saw how many people were there to greet me.

None.

Not Fish.

Not Caleb or Wyatt.

Not even Kenny.

But this was my moment. I had to do something. Coach Harden had come to see a show. I didn't want to disappoint him. So just before I got to the dugout, I looked up, faced the crowd, and I took a bow.

A few people in the stands cheered, but not everyone. I noticed Dad was staring straight ahead, and he wasn't smiling. Maybe he'd missed it.

"That'll show them," I said to Kenny as I took off the batting helmet and laid it on the ground in front of the bench.

"I think the home run was enough," Kenny said.

"What's that supposed to mean?" I asked.

"I'm just saying it wouldn't hurt you to take it easy," he said. "The other guys already think you have an ego. If you keep proving them right, this team is never going to come together."

"We have a four-run lead," I told Kenny. "I'm not going to say I'm sorry for that."

We didn't have a four-run lead for long.

It all fell apart in the top of the fifth inning, when Shane asked if he could pitch. And Coach Darby let him!

"Coach," I said. "Caleb is pitching well. I think we should let him finish."

"I'm sure Shane will do just fine," said Coach.

But Shane didn't do fine. Facing his first batter, he went into a big, loopy windup. I watched helplessly as the ball sailed over the batter's head.

"Hey, everybody!" Julian yelled from second base. "It's the worst pitcher in the world."

That just made Shane pitch worse. His next one was a sidearm toss that hit the dirt in front of Luther, bounced off his glove, and skipped all the way to the backstop. By then he couldn't even keep a straight face.

Things went from bad to worse. It was like a cough going around a classroom. As soon as one person started acting like a clown, everyone else did too. Well, almost everyone else. Caleb, Wyatt, and Kenny were just standing and watching.

When the batter popped up to third base, McKlusky tried to catch the ball in his hat. Then Julian pulled his pants above his waist and smacked his lips. "Hi there, sonny boy," he said.

My teammates were humiliating themselves. And they didn't even care. It was pathetic. By the time the game ended, we had lost by five runs. We were 0–3.

Fish passed me after we had slapped hands with the Reds. "Looks like the scout wasn't very impressed," he said, pointing to the bleachers.

I looked at the spot where Fish had pointed and saw right away what he meant. Walking slowly down the path with his back to the field was Coach Harden. And he was shaking his head.

Anger, frustration, and embarrassment all rushed up from somewhere deep in my gut like chemicals that should never be mixed. I was a science experiment gone wrong. I dug my fingernails into my glove, then hurled it against the metal fence.

Mr. Downer stopped me as soon as I came into the room on Monday and said, "Up front, Mr. Morelli."

I looked at the empty seat he was pointing to. "What do you mean?" I asked.

"From now on, you're going to sit in the front row, where I can see you."

"Why? What did I do?"

"It's what you didn't do," he said, holding up my test, which had a D+ above my name. "You didn't take this test seriously. Now I'm moving you so you'll pay attention."

I slumped into my new seat, dejected. I'd bombed this test the same way I'd bombed the one before it! It was official, I was never going to be good at history.

After the bell rang, I grabbed my bag and headed for the door. Valerie caught up with me at my locker. "Hey," she said. "You wanna walk to the library?"

I was about to say yes, when there was a commotion a few lockers away. I looked over to see Ruben and Derek surrounded by a pack of people. They were talking about a game they'd won last night.

"We're in the last inning, right?" Ruben was saying. "When D comes up and—"

"*Pop!*" Derek said, pretending to hit a baseball. He gazed up at the ceiling, then said, "Home run! Game over!"

That should be me, I thought, watching them celebrate. Suddenly I wanted to be alone. "I just remembered I'm not going straight to the library. Sorry."

"Okay. Well, see you there, I guess."

Valerie seemed annoyed that I didn't want to walk with her, but at that moment, I just wanted to be alone. Without another word, I bolted out the nearest exit and into the afternoon sunshine.

During tutoring that afternoon, I hoped nobody would mention the test, but Valerie, who had gotten a B, couldn't keep her big mouth shut.

"Congratulations," Camille said. "What worked for you?"

"Well," Valerie said, like she had just been crowned

Miss Pilchuck, "I already sit near the front, so that didn't make a difference. But taking notes *definitely* did. I also read for an hour every day."

"Excellent!" Camille said, and high-fived her. "How did you do, Roy?"

"I got a D-plus, okay?" I said, wanting to get it over with.

"I'm surprised to hear that," Camille replied. "Let's think about what went wrong. Did you takes notes and read each night?"

"Maybe not every night," I said, wishing I could be somewhere more fun, like the dentist's office, or in a cage with a hungry lion.

Camille scanned my test. She pointed to the answers I had gotten wrong. "Did you think you knew them when you answered them? Or were you guessing?"

"Mostly guessing," I admitted.

"What about the ones you got right?"

"Those too," I said, going from annoyed to embarrassed.

"I appreciate the honesty, Roy. The good news is you still have time. Plus, you have a lot of people who are here to help."

To me that sounded like there were a lot of people who were going to bug me about this until my head exploded, but I kept that to myself. For the rest of the hour, we reviewed a chapter about the beginning of the Civil War. When we were done, I left quickly, before I had to answer any more questions. I'd have plenty of that to do at home.

I handed the test over as soon as I walked into the kitchen.

Mom rubbed her forehead and looked fed up. I knew she still needed to change out of her work clothes and then go to class. "What happened, Roy? How did you get *another* D? I thought you'd been studying."

"I *did* study," I said. "Every night."

Mom grabbed my chin. "Roy Morelli, look me in the eye and tell me the truth. Did you study for that history test or not?"

I shook my head.

"What did Camille say?" Mom asked.

"She said it looked like I was guessing on most of the questions."

"Were you?"

"I guess so," I muttered.

"Why were you guessing?" Mom snapped. "And don't mumble."

"I was guessing because I didn't know the answers, okay? Why can't everyone just accept that I'm not good at history and that I'm not going to get any better?"

Mom took a minute to gather her thoughts. "Roy, imagine one of your teammates was having a hard time with something, like hitting. Would you tell him that he might as well give up?"

"No," I admitted.

"What would you tell him?"

"I'd tell him if he practiced, he'd get better, but that it might take a while."

Mom exhaled. "So why on earth would I accept the fact that you're not good at history and aren't going to improve?"

"Okay," I said, giving in. "I get it. I need to work harder." Not that I thought it would make any difference.

"A lot harder. Starting tonight. You're going to read for an hour, and then you're going to tell me what you learned. I'm going to quiz you, and if I don't like the answers, you're going to go back to your room and read the chapter again. Understood?"

Just then, the door to the living room swung open and Sara came into the kitchen. She was wearing headphones and carrying a stack of books. She barely noticed me or Mom.

But Mom noticed her. "You," she said, pointing at Sara. "Stop right there. I want to talk to you."

"Can I go?" I asked, before Mom turned back to Sara.

"You can go to your room and study," she said.

In a flash, I left the kitchen, where Mom had cornered Sara. "Didn't I ask you to help your brother get ready for his test?"

"He *told* me he was ready," Sara protested. "What was I supposed to do?"

"You were supposed to make sure, Sara. I was counting on you."

"It's not my fault he—"

I leaned closer to catch the end of the sentence. What was Sara going to say? That I was terrible at history? That I couldn't pass a history test if my life depended on it?

But Mom cut Sara off and said, "You're an excellent student, sweetie, and we're very proud of you, but when you're good at something, you sometimes have to be there for people who need help. Even your brother."

They were interrupted by a phone ringing. "Can I get this?" I heard Sara ask.

"Go ahead," Mom said. "But don't leave the house. I need you to take a casserole out of the oven in forty minutes."

"Got it," Sara said. Then she flipped open her phone. "Hi, Iz. . . . Wait. . . . He did *what* . . . ?"

I slipped into my room and flopped on my bed. I felt like I was on the bottom of the ocean with a trillion pounds of water pressing down on me. Even with help from Camille, Mom, Sara, and everyone else on the planet, I didn't see how I was ever going to pass history. I didn't like it. I wasn't good at it. And as far as I could tell, nothing was going to change that.

· 18 ·

I was reading from my history book on Tuesday night when Mom knocked on my door. "Yes," I said. "I'm studying. You don't have to check up on me every ten minutes."

"No," she said, poking her head in. "It's your dad. Take a break and talk to him."

"Dad?" I said, after I'd picked up the phone.

"Hey, pal. Your mom told me you're hard at work, so I'll make it quick. . . ."

Please, I wanted to say. *Take your time.*

But Dad got right to the point. "What are you doing Saturday after your game?" he asked.

I felt a jolt of excitement. Maybe Dad was going to take me to the batting cages, or out for pizza. A night out with Dad was exactly what I needed.

"Nothing," I said, eager to hear what the plan was.

"Well, Camille and I are going away for a few days next week, and I thought it would be fun to get together before we left. What do you say?"

What do I say? How about . . . I'd rather scrub Moochie Goodman's shoes with my toothbrush than eat dinner with my *history* tutor. But I'd already told Dad I was free that night, so I just said, "Yeah, sure. Sounds great."

"Fantastic," Dad said, obviously much more excited than I was. "And listen, I have to miss your game to do some stuff for work, so Sara will pick you up at the park and bring you to my place. See you then, pal."

Can't wait, I thought, hanging up the phone.

I walked to the game on Saturday with Wyatt and McKlusky.

When we got to the field, we went straight to the dugout. Behind us, Julian was lounging in the bleachers with Fish and Shane. "I don't know about you guys," Julian said, "but I wouldn't want to walk here with Morelli. He'd probably tell me I was doing it wrong."

"Hey, Wyatt," Shane called. "Did you put your shoes on yourself, or did Roy do it for you?"

"Just ignore them," I said to Wyatt. But I was thinking it was pretty lame for Julian and Shane to be picking on their own teammate, and even lamer that Fish was watching it happen.

It got even worse. In the last inning, we were only down a run. But Julian and Luther were sitting on either side of Wyatt, playing keep-away with his hat. It ticked me off, especially since the game wasn't over, so I decided to do something about it.

"Give him his hat back," I said.

Julian ignored me, so I stood up, walked down the bench, and snatched the hat off his head.

"Hand it over, All-Star," he said.

I pointed to Wyatt's hat in Julian's hand. "I'll trade you."

Suddenly, Coach Darby poked his head into the dugout. "Wyatt, looks like you're on deck," he said, tapping his clipboard before ducking out of the dugout to coach third base.

Shane handed Wyatt a helmet, but as soon as Wyatt turned it upside down, dirt and pebbles spilled over his head into his hair and over his face.

"Need a batter, Coach," said the umpire.

Wyatt brushed away the dirt as Julian and Luther laughed. His face was red. While Kenny and McKlusky helped Wyatt, I faced down Julian.

"Go ahead, All-Star," he said. "Hit me. I don't care."

"You aren't worth getting kicked off the team for," I said, shoving my way past him. "Even this team."

I followed Wyatt to the on-deck circle. "Don't worry about those guys," I said. "Just think about the game. We have a chance to win this one."

"I'll probably strike out," he muttered.

"If you think like that, you will," I told him, thinking back to what Mom had told Sara about helping people who needed it. "Just shorten your swing and try to make contact."

Caleb was on first and Fish had taken third on an error, but Wyatt was a mess. The bat was shaking in his hands. With two on and two out, he struck out on four pitches.

The game was over. We had lost—again.

"Good cut!" called Coach Darby.

I didn't get it. How could Coach Darby see a good swing where there wasn't one—but *not* see Julian and Shane put dirt in Wyatt's helmet right under his nose? I went up to Coach Darby after the last out. "I thought your only rule was to have fun," I said.

"That's right," said Coach, who was standing between me and the dugout.

I pointed to Wyatt, who was shuffling toward us from the plate with his shoulders slumped. "Does it look like he's having fun?"

"I'll handle it, Roy. I'm the coach."

"If you say so."

"Excuse me?" Coach asked. For the first time all season, I saw the dopey smile disappear from his face. I didn't care that he was mad at me. I was just glad to see he had an emotion besides *happy*.

"We're oh-and-four," I said. "You haven't taught us a

single thing all season. All you do is tell us that winning doesn't matter. But it *does* matter. And if you acted like it did, we might actually win a game."

"That's enough, Roy. My job is to make baseball safe and fun, not to win every game."

I couldn't hold back anymore. I pulled the glove off my hand and stared at Coach. "You're not listening to me," I told him. "I never said win every game. I said win *a* game. Except every time I try to do that, you get mad at *me*, even though they're picking on Wyatt and acting like idiots during the game."

"Is that what's really bothering you, Roy? How some of your teammates are behaving?"

"What's bothering me is that I'm trying to play good baseball and these losers keep making me look bad!"

I pointed to the dugout, expecting to see my teammates busy getting ready to leave. But all eight of them were staring at me.

Things had just gone from bad to worse. I glanced at Kenny, who had a wounded look on his face. His mouth hung slightly open, but no words came out.

"Who are you calling losers?" asked Julian.

I knew there was no taking back what I had said, but I tried to backpedal anyway. "Not losers, like *losers*. Losers, like we're not winning. Fish, you know what I mean. We just need to get better and . . ."

Fish spat out a sunflower seed and shook his head.

"Come on, Kenny," he said. "Let's get out of here." With one look back at me, Kenny grabbed his glove and left the field with Fish.

The others split right after them. The last two to go were Shane and Julian. As they rounded the fence that ended halfway down the third baseline, Shane said, "Why don't you just quit, Morelli?"

· 19 ·

I went into the apartment in a nasty mood. All I wanted to do was go to my room and stare at the ceiling. But Dad was all over me as soon as Sara and I walked in the door.

"Hey, look, it's Roy and Sara!" he said in a super-excited voice that only made me want to disappear faster.

He was in the kitchen—wearing an apron. Camille was sitting on a barstool next to the counter.

"Hi, guys," she said.

"How was the game, pal?" Dad asked.

"I don't want to talk about it," I said, trying to hustle through the kitchen to my room.

"Whoa, whoa, whoa," Dad called. "Hold up. Can you say hello? We have company."

"Hi," I said. "Can I go now?"

Dad shook his head.

I gave him a dead stare, hoping he would read my mind. Hoping he would see that I wanted to be alone. Instead, he made it worse. "Grab a stool," he said. "Dinner will be ready soon."

I took a seat at the counter, praying there wouldn't be any school talk. The last thing I wanted to hear was how I needed to do better and how everyone was there to help me, like Camille with her list. I did my best to relax, but I knew if I heard the word *history* it would be tick, tick, tick . . . *boom!*

I took a sip of soda from the glass Dad handed me. Sara hopped off her stool and followed Camille into the living room, where the two of them began to look at photos on the bookshelf. That was when I noticed a tent, two sleeping bags, a gas stove, and a pile of clothes sitting next to the brown chair. "What's all that stuff?" I asked.

Dad answered without turning away from the oven. "Camille and I went shopping. We're going to be camping for a few nights and needed some new gear."

"You went shopping today?" I asked. "I thought you were working."

"Well, it was a little of both," Dad said, looking flustered. "But tell me about your game. You can help me set the table too."

While we laid out the knives and forks, I gave Dad a

recap, like I used to do after my All-Star games. I left out the part about the Parkside guys picking on Wyatt, but I told him about all my at bats and a couple of big plays in the field.

"Any sign of Coach Harden?" Dad asked.

"Not today," I said, feeling more upbeat as Sara and Camille joined us at the table. "But he'll be hearing from me when I get to high school."

"Gotta get that history grade up first, though," Dad said, pointing his fork at me.

I couldn't believe it. Dad had found a way to bring up history in the middle of a conversation about baseball.

"I don't want to talk about history," I said, grinding my knife deeper into the chicken.

"Calm down, pal. Nobody's forcing you to talk about anything. I just want you to remember that before you can worry about making the high school team, you need to deal with your grades."

"Oh really?" I said sarcastically. "I need to work harder in history? Thanks so much for pointing that out."

"Knock off the attitude, Roy," Dad said sharply. "We have a guest at the table."

Sara quickly changed the subject. "So, um, Camille, did you always want to be a history teacher?"

Camille smiled gratefully. "Well, I guess I've always been a history buff. The summer I turned twelve, I even passed up two weeks at horse camp to visit my grandparents in Virginia, just because they lived near Monticello. I was kind of a nerd."

It was a relief to be out of the spotlight. I chewed my food and hoped nobody would speak to me again. But apparently Dad just couldn't resist.

Reaching over to squeeze Camille's hand, he said, "Well, I'm just glad you're here now to help Roy." Then he looked at me. "Right, pal?"

"What?" I grumbled.

"I was just telling Camille how lucky we are to have her in our lives."

"Yeah, I've always wanted a tutor who doubled as my dad's girlfriend."

"Jeez, Roy," said Sara. "Take it easy."

Camille pushed her chair away from the table. "I'm going to excuse myself for a moment," she said quietly. She put her hand on the back of Dad's chair. "Mike?"

"Dad," Sara said. "You're blocking Camille."

But Dad was too focused on me to realize Camille couldn't get past him. "That's enough, Roy. I mean it."

"Oh, like you meant it when you said we were going to play baseball, but you went to the art museum instead."

"I'm sorry about that, pal," Dad said calmly as he stood up to let Camille hurry by him. "I made a mistake. I just wish you would see that I'm happy and maybe cut me some slack."

"Did it ever occur to you that some of us were happy *before* you got a girlfriend? Or have you just been waiting for someone to come along and change you into someone you're not?"

"I'm still the same person. I'm still your father."

"No way," I said. "*My* father doesn't pick shopping over a baseball game. *My* father doesn't make his kid play in the rec league just because he got a bad grade on a test. *My* father doesn't read history books just to impress some woman."

Camille was at the door now. "Um, I think I should go," she said.

Dad shook his head. "No, wait."

Camille stayed where she was.

But I didn't. I got up from the table and shoved my chair aside. I slipped past Camille, who had her head down, and stepped through the door.

Dad caught up to me at the top of the stairs that led to the parking lot. He put his hand on my shoulder. "What do you think is going on here?" he asked. "Who do you think Camille is to me? Do you think I would bring her into your life and Sara's life if she was just some woman?"

"She's not coming into my life," I said. "She's coming into yours. And I don't want her help *anymore*." I broke free from Dad's grip and sprinted down the stairs. I was gone.

* * *

I was halfway home when headlights came up from behind me. I didn't look back. I wasn't getting in a car with Dad. But it was Sara calling my name. "Get in," she said. "I'll take you home."

Seeing she was alone, I hopped into the car. I slumped against the window. Music was playing through the speakers. We were quiet for a few blocks.

"He should've stuck to baseball," Sara finally said as she drove through Pilchuck.

"Tell me about it," I said.

We didn't say another word, which was fine with me. In fact, it was more than fine. It was a relief, for once. At least *she* knew it.

"Your father called," Mom said when we got home. "He said you can call anytime tonight. I guess they're leaving early tomorrow morning and won't be easy to reach for a few days after that. Is everything all right?"

"No," I said. "But I don't want to talk about it. I just want to go to sleep."

"Sure, sweetie," Mom said. "I'm always here."

I headed to my room and crashed on the bed, ready to forget everything that had happened that night.

· 20 ·

I was sitting in my front-row seat after the bell rang on Monday. Fish and Kenny had just walked out of the room together when a wad of paper hit me on the side of my head. It bounced off my desk and onto the floor. I turned around to see Valerie standing up with her arm extended.

"Gotcha," she said.

"Yeah, yeah," I replied. "We're even."

"Oh, come on, Health Hazard," she said. "Where's your sense of humor?"

"You never thought I was funny before," I reminded her, dropping my book into my bag.

"True," she agreed. "But you did make life interesting. Now you just ignore me."

"I'm not ignoring you," I said, pulling myself out of my seat. "I've just been, I don't know, busy."

"You don't look busy right now."

"I guess you'd know."

We were standing there with a poster of Lewis and Clark between us. Out in the hallway, I could see the rest of the Social Committee huddled around a locker. Any second, Valerie was going to lose interest in me and join her friends.

But Valerie leaned against the wall with her shoulder on Clark's face. Or maybe it was Lewis. "We could get some pizza," she said.

"Very funny."

"No, I'm serious," she said. "Camille's gone, so there's no tutoring, and you look like you could use a slice. My treat."

"I thought you were out of my league."

Valerie sauntered through the door. "I am." She waved goodbye to her friends and led the way out of the school.

Corner Pizza was dead. It figured. Everyone was probably following Ruben and Derek around town. Valerie chose a table near the window, and we sat down with our slices. One cheese for her. Two Hawaiian for me.

"So why are you moping around like it's the end of the world? Is it all about school?" She narrowed her eyes. "Is it about me?"

"You wish," I said.

"Is it not sitting next to Fish and Kenny?"

"More like the opposite," I said. "Ever since I joined their baseball team, Fish has been acting like he's too good for me. He's hanging around with these Parkside clowns. And now Kenny's freezing me out too, even though the whole thing was his idea. I don't know why they're so mad. I mean, they should be happy to have me on the team."

"You don't say things like *that* around them, do you?"

"What?" I said. "It's not a lie. If I was good enough for the All-Star team, I'm definitely good enough for *their* team. But somehow I'm the odd man out, which is going to be tons of fun next year." I took a sip of my soda. I couldn't believe how much I had told her. If Valerie thought I had problems before, I wondered what she'd think now.

"What do you mean?" she asked.

"A month ago, I was set. I was going to roll into high school. I was going to hang out with the baseball team. I had it all worked out. Now I've got squat. I'm going to be one of those kids who hangs out with the janitors."

"What about Kenny and Fish?" Valerie asked.

"I told you. They're blowing me off too."

"I don't know about you, Health Hazard, but I can tell when one of my friends thinks I'm a backup. They start talking about all these big plans they have. And I'm not in them. So if I was Kenny and Fish and you were blah, blah, blahing about the high school team all the time, I'd pick up on it. Then I'd make sure I had my own backups."

"Then you're using someone, just like someone else used you."

"That's how it goes," said Valerie.

"Nice," I said.

"Cheer up, Roy. It's not too late. You're on the same baseball team, right? Just let them know how you feel."

"How am I supposed to do that?"

"I don't know," said Valerie. "Go up and punch one of them, or whatever it is boys do."

We were quiet for a minute. Valerie wiped her hands. I finished my soda. My throat was dry from talking so much.

"So, is your team any good?" Valerie asked.

"No," I said. "They're not. We're not. I mean, I am. So are a couple other guys. But the rest of them, they don't even try. I don't even know why they're on the team. Every time I see them, they're laughing and joking around. And the coach lets them get away with it because he just wants everyone to have fun."

"It sounds like they are," said Valerie.

"Are what?"

"Having fun. You said they're always laughing and

joking around. That's what people do when they're having fun. Maybe that's why they're on the team."

"It's not fun if we don't win," I said.

"Yeah, to you. But not to them." Valerie held up her hands. "Look, I don't really care that much, and don't take this the wrong way, but you're the last person who should be talking about not trying right now." I opened my mouth, but she cut me off. "Don't make me explain it, Roy. You know what I'm talking about."

"That's different. History is hard," I said. "You needed tutoring too. And that wasn't all my fault."

"It was mostly your fault," she said. "Anyway, the Roy Morelli I *thought* I knew wouldn't just give up because something wasn't easy."

Later that evening, back in my room, I thought about my conversation with Valerie and wondered if she was right. *Had* I given up in history? And was that just as bad as not even trying, like some of my teammates? If so, then I was a major league hypocrite.

I lay down on my bed and tried to figure out how all this had happened. A month ago, I couldn't wait to be a big shot at a high school with nine hundred sixty-seven people. Now it scared the pants off me. I still wanted to play for Coach Harden, but not as much as I wanted to be friends with Kenny and Fish.

Even worse, none of that would matter if I didn't

pass Mr. Downer's history class. So that night, I sat at my desk, I opened my book, and I began to read, line by line, page by page. I came across a section about Dred Scott—how he was a slave who sued for his freedom, but lost his case because the judge ruled that any state could be a slave state. I took notes, but I didn't know if it made any difference. I hoped it would, though, because I needed to light up the scoreboard on the final, and I was running out of time.

• 21 •

In class on Wednesday, Mr. Downer pointed his ruler at me. Picking up where Derek had stopped, I read from a chapter about the war with Mexico. It had been more than a week since Mr. Downer had moved me, and even though I missed the old days of bagball and thumb wars, I had to admit one thing. It was a lot easier to follow along from the front row.

After the bell rang, Mr. Downer gestured for me to stop at his desk. "You wanted to see me?" I asked, wondering what I could have done wrong now.

"Yes," said Mr. Downer. "I wanted to tell you that your behavior in this class has improved significantly. You haven't caused a disturbance in nearly a month."

Wow, I thought, genuinely surprised. Had it really been that long? "Um, you're welcome?"

"Keep it up," he said with a grin. "Participation counts, and you need all the help you can get."

It felt good to get a compliment from Mr. Downer. But my mood went south again when I saw Fish and Kenny leaving the room together. I hadn't spoken to either of them since the end of the last game. I knew I was ready to make peace, but I wasn't sure how to do it. As I walked to practice that day by myself, I was still trying to figure it all out.

Fish and Kenny weren't the only ones I needed to clear the air with.

I found Coach Darby alone at the ball field before practice. He was lining up the bats against the fence. "I'm sorry, Coach," I told him. "I shouldn't have said what I said on Saturday. I didn't mean it."

Coach brushed his hands together, sending a cloud of dust into the air. "Thank you, Roy. I appreciate that."

"I hope you won't kick me off the team."

"I was tempted," he said. "But that wouldn't have been right. Because you weren't entirely wrong."

"I wasn't?"

"No. You have high expectations for yourself, and you aren't afraid to let the rest of us know it. I admire that." He gave me a stern look. "Don't get me wrong. I don't like the way you handled it when you got frustrated. You were disrespectful. You should have come to me earlier, man to man, and told me how you felt. But I know the frustration was coming from a good place, and I hope you won't think twice about speaking your mind again. Because if you kids did everything exactly the way we told you to, you wouldn't learn anything about yourselves. You know what I mean?"

"I think so."

"You should also know that I spoke to Julian, Luther, and Shane after the game about their behavior. They know they were wrong to do it, and I know I was wrong not to stop it earlier."

Coach finished with the bats, then opened a bag and began pulling out batting helmets. I was relieved that he and I had made peace, but I was still worried about the rest of the team.

"Do . . . do you think I'm a show-off?" I asked, cringing as the words came out.

He shook his head. "I think that's your way of having fun," he said. "You crossed the line when you took a bow, but on the field, no, I don't think you're a show-off."

Hearing that gave me the courage to ask another question. "Do you think the guys hate me?"

"*Hate*'s a strong word. I think you all just got off on the wrong foot. You gave them about as much of a chance as they gave you." He made a circle with his fingers. "Zippo."

"I didn't mean anything by it," I said. "I was just trying to play my best. I was trying to . . ."

"Impress Bull Harden?"

My eyes flew open. "You know about that?"

"I have eyes, Roy. I saw him in the stands. I knew he wasn't there to see me."

"I hope he comes back," I said, excited that Coach Darby had noticed the Bull too.

"Can I give you some advice? Just in case he does come back."

I nodded eagerly. "Sure."

"Sometimes a scout learns more by watching the players around the guy he's scouting than he does by watching the guy himself."

"So the team *is* making me look bad."

"They don't make you look bad because they're not as talented as you, Roy. They make you look bad because they don't trust you. Because you don't trust them. If you want them to help you make a better impression, you need to start making them feel good around you. That's what a leader does. And that's what a coach likes to see."

"But the guys don't want to win, and even if they did, I'm not sure they could."

By then, the other players were arriving. Wyatt showed up, sticking close to McKlusky. Kenny and Fish appeared together. Caleb came alone. Finally, the Parkside guys walked up in a pack.

"I've gotta get something out of my car," Coach said with a wink. "I might be a few minutes. Just talk to them, Roy."

Slowly, my teammates gathered around me. Some of them were looking at me like I had two choices: I could leave the field on my own, or they would make me leave.

"I thought we told you to quit," Julian said.

"Sorry," I said. "I'm not a quitter."

"Neither are we," said Luther.

"Yeah," said Shane. "We're just trying to have a good time. And you're ruining it."

"Maybe we don't want exactly the same things," I said. "But we need each other."

"We'll have fun with or without you," Shane said. "But you need us to win."

"But I'm not the only one who wants to win," I said. "In fact, I bet there are more of us than there are of you. And if we don't start playing better, this season won't be fun for *anyone*."

"Quit trying to scare us," said Julian. "This isn't a pirate ship. There isn't going to be a mutiny."

"Yeah," Luther said. "Besides, we have four games left. We might win one of them. We might win all of them."

"Don't make me laugh," I said. "You haven't won a game in two years. You just go on pretending it doesn't matter to make yourselves feel better."

Fish forced his way to the front of the pack. "You are so full of it," he said. "You never cared about whether we won. You've acted like you were better than us from the second you got here. All you cared about was looking good in front of Coach Harden."

"So you started bossing us around," said Julian. "Because you were afraid we'd make you look bad. Or did I hear you wrong?"

Caleb looked at Fish angrily. "You don't know what you're talking about, Fishman. Roy has been playing to win since the first game. So don't—"

"No," I cut in. "He's right. I was trying to impress Coach Harden. And I was playing like I was still on the All-Star team. But you guys were playing like every game was a big joke. And if you ask me, that's just as bad."

"We didn't ask you what you thought," Julian said, still scowling. "So why don't you keep your opinions to yourself?"

"It's not just his opinion," said Caleb. "It's mine too. You guys are keeping this team from winning. And it's not fair to the rest of us."

Shane jabbed his finger at me. "If you two don't like the way we play, then maybe you should start your own team."

"Touch me again," I dared him.

"Back off, Shane," said Caleb.

Shane didn't budge. "Make me."

Before I knew what was happening, Caleb had bumped Shane, which set everyone off. There was a lot of shoving and shouting. Kenny wormed his way in and tried to break it up, but got pushed aside.

Fish glared at me from across the tangle of bodies. "You see what you did, Roy? You turned the whole team against itself! All because you didn't get what you wanted."

"Quit blaming me for everything!" I yelled back. "It's your bonehead friends who cause all the problems!"

Things were boiling over now. I thought any minute someone was going to get decked. Then, just before it got completely out of hand, a voice ripped through the pack.

"Everyone shut up and listen!"

Almost instantly, the melee ended. We looked around to see where the voice had come from. And there, standing by himself, was Wyatt.

"Everyone on this team needs to stop fighting," he said. "We're not All-Stars, Roy, so deal with it."

"Yeah," said Shane.

"But this is a baseball team," Wyatt told Shane. "And the last time I checked, the point of playing baseball was to *win the game.* But all we do is lose and pretend we like it. Well, I'm sick of it. I'm sick of being the worst team in the league. And we're not going to get any better without Roy. He might be all those things you say he is, but he sticks up for his teammates, which is more than I can say for the rest of you. So I say we try it his way." Then he walked right up to Julian and Shane. "One more thing. The next time you guys put dirt in my helmet, I'll break it over your heads. You got that?"

"Hold on a minute," Luther said. "I thought we already voted not to do any of Roy's drills."

"Yeah," said Julian. "And we won, six to three."

"Well, I'm changing my vote," Wyatt said. "So now it's five to four."

There were two people who still hadn't revoted: Kenny and Fish. At the moment, Fish was standing with the Parkside guys, and Kenny was on his own. I saw Kenny glance over at Fish, but Fish's eyes were fixed on the distance, shutting out everyone.

For a second, nobody spoke. I was beginning to worry that I really had destroyed the team.

At last, Kenny broke the silence. Looking at Fish, he said, "I'm not taking sides here, but I think we need to start something different. So I say we do some drills."

This time, there was no cheering after the final vote, like there had been a few weeks ago. Instead, Julian came up to me and said, "If we do it your way, then you gotta change too. No more telling us what to do. And no more showing us up on the field."

"Or the other team," said Wyatt.

"And," Kenny added, "you gotta play for *us,* not for Coach Harden."

I stuck out my hand. "It's a deal."

· 22 ·

When the dust settled, the first person I looked for was Fish. I found him at the drinking fountain on the far side of the bleachers. "Are we cool?" I asked.

With a shrug, Fish gave me a weak handshake.

"Come on, Fish," I said. "It'll be different. I promise. This isn't about the high school team."

"Don't lie," he said.

"I'm not lying," I said. "I swear. From now on, it's all about our team."

Fish laughed. "Why don't you just admit it? You'll never be *all* about our team. It's not who you are. Can you really look me in the eye and tell me that you don't care about impressing Coach Harden?"

There was no use pretending Fish was wrong. He was one of my best friends. He knew me too well.

"Okay," I said. "You're right. I do care about Coach Harden. I care a lot. I want to be on the high school team more than anything."

"But you just promised everyone you were going to play for us."

"I know what I said, Fish."

"So which is it? Is it him or is it us?"

"It's both!" I said. "All right? It's both. I want the team to win a game *and* I want to make the high school team. What's so wrong about wanting something for myself?"

"Nothing," said Fish. "But if that's all you want, then we got problems."

"It isn't," I said. "I'm telling you, one guy to another, that it isn't. And I'm sorry if I acted like a jerk. I didn't mean it."

Fish stuck his hand out for real. "Okay," he said. "*Now* we're cool."

"Yeah?"

"Yeah," he said. "And I'm sorry too."

"For what?" I asked.

"For ditching you for the Parkside guys."

"You didn't teach them bagball, did you?"

"I tried to, but they weren't very good." He smiled. "You know, since they can't throw straight."

When I walked into the kitchen after practice, Mom was rinsing out a pan and Sara was sitting at the table, tapping the keys on her phone so rapidly I could barely see her fingers move. "Dad called," she said without looking up.

I leaned against the counter. "What did he say?"

"He said you're a loose cannon with an attitude problem and an overinflated ego."

"He did not, Sara," Mom scolded. "Sweetie, he said he loves you very much and he can't wait to see you tomorrow."

I smiled after hearing that. I was looking forward to seeing him too, even if I'd stepped in it the last time we were together.

"Did you have a good practice?" Mom asked.

"Actually we had a huge fight and I almost destroyed the team," I said.

"Is everything okay?" Mom asked, sounding concerned.

"Better than ever," I assured her. "I just wish I didn't have to wait three days for the next game."

"Well, maybe you can make the time go faster by studying for your history test."

"I *have* been studying, Mom."

"Okay," she said. "Pop quiz. Who was president before Lincoln?"

I didn't think about it. I just said the first name that popped into my head. "Buchanan."

"Is that right?" Mom asked Sara.

"It shocks me to say it is," Sara replied.

It shocked me too.

"Let me try one," Sara said. "Why did the colonists oppose the Stamp Act?"

The who and the what? No, wait. I knew what all those words meant. I just had to remember how they went together.

"Ehhhh!" said Sara, hitting the table like it was a buzzer. "Time's up. Better luck next time."

"Hit the books," Mom said, rubbing the top of my head. "You only have three weeks until the final."

"Don't remind me," I said, going to my room. I would have a better chance of hitting a home run in a major league stadium than I did of passing that test. I knew I needed Camille's help now more than ever.

Just before history class began on Thursday, a seventh grader with a hall pass brought a note to Mr. Downer. "The secretary gave you this?" he asked.

"Yup," said the seventh grader, glancing at the door. "Can I go now?"

Mr. Downer nodded, then called out, "Mr. Morelli and Ms. Hopkins, this is for you. It's from your . . . tutor?" He looked at the note again. "You have a tutor?"

"Yes, sir," I said, actually feeling proud that I did.

"That explains a lot," he replied.

I unfolded the note on my desk so Valerie and I could read it.

Roy and Valerie,
   Meet me at the cemetery
today at 3:00. We have work
to do.
                              Camille

Valerie and I looked at each other. "The cemetery?"
she said, looking a little spooked. "Why would she
want to meet us there?"

"Beats me. But it's better than the library."

Valerie shivered momentarily. "Speak for yourself."
Suddenly she snapped her fingers. "Uh-oh. I don't
think I can make it. My mom is taking me to pick up
the invitations for the graduation party. Do you think
Camille will be mad?"

"I doubt it. I mean, I need a lot more help than you."

"That's true," said Valerie. "Hey, I thought Camille
was out of town."

"She is," I said. "They get back today."

"They?" she asked. "Who's they?"

"Oh yeah, I forgot to tell you. Camille is kind of going out with my dad."

Valerie's eyes bulged. "I can't believe you," she said as
the bell rang. "You said you knew her through your sister. But she's your dad's *girlfriend*. Oh, that explains *so*
much," she said, just before Mr. Downer started class.

Valerie walked with me to the cemetery. She said it

was on her way home. We stuck to the sunny side of the road as we made our way from school.

"Slow down," Valerie said. "I can barely keep up with you."

"Sorry. I just don't want to keep Camille waiting."

"Right, because you're such a gentleman." Valerie chuckled at her own joke, then asked, "So, do you like her?"

"Who?"

"Camille. Do you like her? I mean, not as a tutor. But as, you know . . ."

"My dad's girlfriend?"

"Yeah."

"I don't really know her that well," I admitted. "I think she's made my dad do some weird stuff. But I guess she's okay."

"I remember when my mom first started dating Mark—he's my stepdad now—I didn't like him very much. I probably wasn't very nice to him."

"Hard to imagine," I said.

Valerie punched my shoulder. "Ha-ha," she said. "*Any*way, once I got over all the 'don't take my mom away' and 'you're not my dad' stuff, I realized he wasn't so bad. I guess the worst thing was that nobody ever asked me. It was just one day, there's this guy in the living room and he's holding my mom's hand with this look on his face like he wants to kiss her. But what was I supposed to do? Close my eyes and wish that nothing would ever change? Unlikely." Valerie paused to catch her breath. "So what does she make your dad do that's so weird?"

"Little things, I guess. He took her to an art museum one day when we were supposed to play baseball."

"That's it?" said Valerie.

"Also, you should see this book she got him to read. *History of People* or something."

"Does she have kids?"

"Not that I know of."

"Then stop complaining. When you have step-siblings, call me. Otherwise, count your blessings."

"They're that bad?"

"Not bad," Valerie said as we reached the iron gate. "Just not easy." She looked into the cemetery. "Well, this is as far as I go today. You're on your own, Health Hazard."

Camille showed up a few minutes later. "Hi, Roy. Is it just you?"

"Valerie couldn't make it," I said. "Um, how was your trip?"

"It was nice," she said, smiling nervously. "Did you have a good week in school?"

"Mr. Downer says I've been paying attention in class."

"Have you?"

"Actually, yeah. I mean, it's harder to get in trouble when you're sitting in the front row," I said, trying to break the ice with a joke.

"Roy," Camille said, "I want you to know, if this is too complicated . . . if you'd rather have a tutor who . . ." She paused, searching for the right words.

"Isn't going out with my dad?"

"Right," she said. "If that's making it uncomfortable, then I'm sure we could find someone to help you until the end of the school year."

I took a deep breath and looked Camille in the eyes. "I don't want a new tutor. And I'm sorry about the stuff I said at dinner. I want you to help me with history, because I, um, really need it."

"I'd like that, Roy," Camille said with a big smile. "Thank you." Then she looked at her watch. "Ready to get started?"

"Ready," I said.

Camille led me past rows and rows of graves, from new headstones with the shine still on the names to older stones faded by weather. After a while, we had gone back in time to graves of people who had died before my parents were born. 1950s, 1940s, 1930s. No more flowers or American flags or anything like that. These graves hadn't been visited in a long, long time. We were out of the 1900s and into the 1800s when Camille stopped under a leafy oak tree.

"So how are you feeling about the final test?" she asked, reaching down and picking up a pinecone.

"Not real good," I admitted.

"Why not?" she asked.

"Well, I'm doing most of the stuff you said to do. I'm sitting in the front row. I've started reading every night. I'm not memorizing anything. But my sister asked me a question yesterday that I should have known and I totally froze. I knew what all the words meant. I just couldn't say how they all went together."

Camille nodded. "Believe me, I get it. Dead presidents, dead explorers, dead pioneers. You start to wonder if they ever took a breath." She paused as a squirrel ran up an oak tree. "You're probably also wondering why I asked you to come to a cemetery."

"Sort of."

"I know it's weird," Camille said. "But I thought coming here might make the idea of history a bit less intimidating. You see, Roy, I know it seems like everything you're studying happened a million years ago, but this country, it isn't that old."

I looked around at the crumbling graves. "It feels old."

Camille was getting excited now. "Do you know how few years have actually passed since the Constitution was signed?"

"Two hundred and . . . um, something."

"It's less than three lifetimes!" Camille said.

"What do you mean?" I asked.

Camille pointed to a nearby headstone. "Read the years that person lived."

I squinted, then read, "1875 to 1975."

"Now read the name."

"Henry McClure."

Camille nodded. "That's my great-grandfather. He died when I was five years old. But before he died, he told me a story about *his* grandmother Abigail. When she was a little girl, she lived at Mount Vernon. Her mother was a servant there. Anyway, President Washington liked Abigail so much that he took her for a ride on his favorite horse. At least, that's how the story goes."

For a moment, I could see George Washington up close. Not as a general or a president, not in a book or on a dollar bill, but as an old man with bad breath and a rattling cough. Like Mr. Downer—with a wig, and taller.

"So you knew someone who knew someone who knew George Washington," I said. "I guess it wasn't that long ago after all."

Camille pushed a few curls of hair off her forehead. "Exactly, Roy. Those people in your book, they haven't been gone that long. And I think if you thought of them as real people, instead of names you have to re-member for a test, they might be a bit more inter-esting."

"Very cool," I said, stepping away from Henry McClure's grave. "A little creepy, but definitely better than the book. But how does that help me on the test?"

"History is about dates and names," Camille replied. "There's no getting around that. But it's also about cause and effect. It's about understanding *why* all those people did what they did. And what happened because of what they did." She tossed the pinecone aside. "Look, Roy, there was a moment in the library when you *were* Dred Scott. You were thinking like him. You knew where he was from, what he wanted, and why he wanted it. And you weren't memorizing. You were making an argument."

"I was?"

"Let's try something," she said. "Go back to being Dred Scott."

Camille was so full of energy, I was actually happy to go along with it. "Okay," I said, trying to imagine I was a slave. "I'm Dred Scott."

"What do you want, Dred?" she asked.

"My freedom," I said, imagining what it would be like to work for someone else because he owned me.

"But you're a slave," Camille pointed out.

"But I lived in a free state."

"Did you tell the judge that?"

"Yes," I said, a little defensively, as though Camille were asking Dred and not me. "I told Judge What's-His-Name. I mean, Taney."

"What did he say?"

I flashed back to the night I had read about the

Dred Scott case in my textbook. "He didn't listen! He said there were no free states or slave states because I was someone's property."

"So what's the big deal?" Camille asked. "You're just one man, right, Dred?"

I could see the notes I had taken like they were on a screen in my head. "Yeah, but if I was still a slave after being in a free state, then the whole deal was off."

"What deal?"

"The North-South thing. The Missouri Compromise. Nobody paid attention to it anymore. It was a free-for-all. Until the Civil War." I stopped talking and looked at Camille. "Is that right?"

"Yes," she said. "That's exactly right. It's all in there, Roy. You just have to think through how it all goes together."

"You make it sound easy. Like if I said all you had to do to get a hit was swing the bat."

"I didn't say it was easy. I said it was interesting. And I don't know about you, but the things I'm good at and the things I enjoy, they tend to be the same. But you still have to put in the work."

We faced each other for a moment as a breeze rustled the leaves of the trees around us. "Your dad told me you want to play for Coach Harden," she said.

"You know who he is?" I asked as we started to walk back to the cemetery gate.

"We do work at the same school, you know."

"Right," I said. "Well, you can tell him Roy Morelli wants another shot."

"Shot at what?" Camille asked.

I explained our history to Camille. The All-Star team. Moochie Goodman. Coach Harden leaving my game shaking his head. Even my new deal with the rest of the team. "I guess you could call it the Pilchuck Compromise," I said.

"Let's hope this one doesn't lead to a Civil War," said Camille.

"That's kind of how it started," I told her as we reached the sidewalk.

"Well," said Camille. "I hope this was helpful."

"It beats the library."

"Good. And you've got the list I made for you, right?"

"I've got it," I said. "But, um, we're not done, are we? I mean, I can still come on Monday, right?"

"Done?" Camille asked. "Roy, you're just getting started."

· 23 ·

When I got home from the cemetery, Dad was waiting out front in his truck. In the bed, along with his tools and a few two-by-fours, was a bat, two gloves, and a bag of balls. "Hop in," he said. "Let's go hit some baseballs."

It was a warm day, even for the middle of May, perfect weather for baseball. But I knew I had to do an hour of reading and my other homework.

"It's okay," Dad said, reading my mind. "I talked to your mom. We've got one hour."

"Really?" I said, excited, but afraid there might be a catch.

"Well," Dad said. "I also promised her you'd do an extra two hours of homework tomorrow at my place."

I knew it! "You *what*?"

"Gotcha!" Dad laughed and pushed the door open. "Clock's ticking."

I climbed into the truck and we were on our way. I decided I didn't want anything hanging over us during batting practice, so I came right out and told Dad how sorry I was. "I never should have said all that stuff about Camille. It wasn't true."

"I'm sorry too," Dad said. "This all happened real quick. Maybe I could have handled it better. I guess I just got swept up. I lost my head." Then he patted me on the knee. "But, Roy. The thing is, I am going to change, and so are you. That's how it goes. I'm going to meet new people, find new interests, go places I've never been. But it doesn't mean how I feel about you or Sara is going to change. It just means I'm living my life. And that's all I want you to do. Are you okay with that?"

"Definitely," I said. "But exactly how many new people are you planning to meet?"

"Not many like Camille," he said.

I thought about my trip to the cemetery with Camille and how cool she had been. "I can live with that too," I told him.

Boardman Park was jammed with people playing baseball, throwing Frisbees, walking their dogs, even sunbathing. But we managed to find an empty field in the back.

When we were done, Dad and I sat in the bleachers and caught our breath. Over on another field, I could see the All-Stars taking batting practice. Moochie was at the plate, his hat turned backward and a gold batting glove on each hand. He was driving balls into the outfield, some of them pretty deep.

"Is that him?" Dad asked. "Mookie . . . the poseur?"

"That's him," I said. "Moochie Goodman."

Dad watched as Moochie finished his turn and took the field. "He's not bad," he said.

"He's a loser. And next year, he's gonna be on the bench. Because I'm playing shortstop for Coach Harden." Of course, it was easier said than done, since I still had to ace the history final, then play better than Moochie in tryouts.

Dad put his arm around me. "Good for you, Roy. I know you can do anything you set your mind to."

Saturday was our first game since the blowup at practice. Coach Darby led off with a pregame speech. "Fellas," he said. "We've got four games left in the season. And starting now, we've got a new team rule."

We were standing in a circle under the warm May sun. I was more excited to play baseball than I had been since the first game of the season. In fact, it felt like the beginning of a *new* season. I wondered what Coach's new rule was.

"Just have fun?" McKlusky guessed.

"No, McKlusky, it's not just have fun. The new team

rule is *let's win one.*" Coach swept his eyes around the circle. He took the time to look straight at each of us.

"You can still have fun. But if you want to win—and I think you do—then we're going to work too. And we're going to play as a team. Because if we don't, we're not going to beat anyone."

Kenny was the first to put his hand out for the cheer. "Let's win one," he said.

Caleb was next. "Let's win one," he said, a little louder.

I slapped my hand down on Caleb's. "Let's win one," I said, feeling the old electricity run through me.

Fish, Wyatt, and McKlusky followed.

That left the Parkside guys. Quick glances bounced from one of them to the next. This was it, I thought. We had made a deal and shaken on it at practice. I was ready to keep up my end—but were they ready to keep up theirs? I saw the rest of the team watching breathlessly, as everyone waited to see what would happen. It was the biggest play of the season, and we weren't even on the field!

Finally, slowly, Julian lifted his hand, then dropped it on the pile. "If we can have fun *and* win, then I'm in," he said.

"Same here," said Luther.

"Let's win one," Shane said with a smile.

I ran out to the field, soaking up the afternoon sun.

"Hey," said Fish, jogging over from third base. "Who's that next to your dad?"

I looked into the bleachers, where Dad was sitting with Camille. "That's his, um, girlfriend," I said. "She's all right."

"That explains why they're holding hands," said Fish, walking back to his position.

"Oh, she's also my history tutor."

Fish turned around with a confused look on his face.

"Don't ask," I said, and smiled.

The Cardinals started the game with a bang. Actually it was a loud ping. The ping of the ball leaving the aluminum bat and disappearing over the wall for a leadoff home run. The game was less than a minute old and we were already losing.

By the bottom of the seventh—our last licks—we were down five runs. Fish batted first that inning. He led off with a single that grazed the top of the first baseman's glove. Shane followed with a walk. After that, Caleb moved Fish and Shane into scoring position with a ground ball to the right side of the infield.

I looked down the bench. Nobody was laughing. Nobody was picking on Wyatt. All I saw were four guys sitting on the edge of their seats, eyes fixed on the game.

Kenny elbowed me. "Two on. We're still in it."

Feeling that not-dead-yet tingle in my hands, I watched Luther go to the plate—and fall behind, 0–2.

That was when I heard McKlusky say, "Hey, Julian, how come you're changing your shoes?"

I turned to see Julian with one cleat off and a sneaker in his right hand. "Because the game is over."

"It's not over," I said. "There's only one out. When there are three outs, then it's over."

The next pitch came. I shut my eyes, ready to hear the umpire call strike three. Instead, what I heard was contact. Solid contact. I opened my eyes. Luther had ripped a single into left field. Fish came around to score. Hot on his heels, Shane slid across the plate.

Kenny clapped to himself as he went to the plate.

Fish came into the dugout, fist pumping.

"Nice slide," I said to Shane, holding out my hand.

Shane paused for a second before offering *his* hand. "Thanks, Morelli," he said, before throwing off his batting helmet. "We can get these guys."

Julian looked up. "Yeah, right. We need, like, five runs and there's already two outs."

Hearing Julian, Coach Darby whipped his head around. "There is *one* out, Julian. And we need three runs, not five. So get your cleats back on and be ready to bat. You got that?"

"This is supposed to be fun?" Julian muttered.

But I was too busy watching Luther run the bases to

answer Julian's question. Kenny had dropped a blooper into left field. Luther took off like a shot, rounded second, then stopped halfway to third, daring the left fielder to make a play. It worked. The left fielder threw to second. But as soon as the ball was in the air, Luther broke for third. The second baseman rushed a throw to third, but it was too late. Luther slid in safely. Even better, the Cardinals were so busy with Luther, they didn't see Kenny sneak into second!

That was what I called baseball!

McKlusky got Luther home with a sac fly. We were down two runs. Wyatt was up, I was on deck, and Julian was in the hole. After Wyatt walked and I singled, the bases were loaded.

Julian took the first pitch for strike one. He stepped away from the plate and sized up the defense.

He fouled back the next pitch. Strike two now. But that only made us cheer louder.

Then, on an 0–2 pitch at the knees, Julian put all his weight into a swing and met the ball with everything he had. Right on the sweet spot.

From first base, I could see the looks on the faces of my teammates as they watched Julian's hit rocket toward the outfield. Their eyes tracked the ball as it rose higher. Their hands clenched the bar. They held their breath.

I knew that look from playing with the All-Stars. My teammates believed we were going to win a game. They *wanted* to win a game.

No matter what happened next, there was no way they could tell me, Coach Darby, each other, or themselves that they didn't care about winning. Because the only thing that made a team want to win more than winning was *almost* winning.

And we *almost* won that day. Julian drove the ball to the warning track, where the center fielder caught it for the final out. The dugout was silent, but it was okay. Because for the first time all season we *all* cared about how the game had ended. Sure, it was brutal to lose like that, but at least nobody was pretending it didn't matter.

· 24 ·

Valerie and I walked to the library together on Monday for our first tutoring session since Camille had taken me to the cemetery.

"Did you know Andrew Jackson fought thirteen duels?" I asked her, remembering something I had read the night before.

"I don't think that's going to be on the test," Valerie said as we made our way to the small room in the back.

"It's still kinda cool," I said. "Can you picture the president standing in the middle of the street firing a pistol at someone now?"

"I guess not," Valerie admitted. "But that might be a good thing."

"No way," I said. "If I have to read about a president, this is the guy for me."

"Which guy?" asked Camille as we got ready to start.

"Andrew Jackson," I said. "He killed someone in a duel for talking trash about his wife."

"He also spent most of his life with a bullet lodged in his chest," Camille added.

"What a gentleman," said Valerie. "We should put him on Mount Rushmore."

"We should put you on Mount Snobmore," I said, cracking myself up.

Valerie rolled her eyes. "We should put you on Mount Dorkmore."

"Why don't we get started?" Camille said, her eyes bouncing back and forth from me to Valerie. She handed us each a stack of note cards.

"What are these for?" I asked.

"You have two weeks and two days until your big test," Camille explained. "What I want you to do between now and then is create flash cards. As you're reading, every time you come across a name, a place, or any term that seems important, write it on one side. On the other side, write down why that term is important."

"That could take forever," I said. "Can't we just *buy* flash cards?"

Camille wagged her finger at me. "No shortcuts, Roy."

The courtyard was packed with people after school on Tuesday. The sun was shining and everyone was wearing T-shirts and shorts. I was sitting in the grass, waiting for Valerie. We had made plans to go back to the library together.

"Hey, Morelli," said Derek, sauntering up with Ruben at his side. "What's up?"

"What's up with you guys?" I asked.

"We're going to the high school," Ruben said. "Coach Harden told us we could take some cuts in batting practice. You wanna go?"

I felt my whole body spasm for a moment. My heart began to pound. I could practically feel the bat in my hands already. I wondered how many people Coach Harden had invited. "Who else is going?" I asked.

"Just us," Derek said.

"Not Moochie?"

"Nah," Ruben said. "We were gonna ask him, but that guy never stops talking."

"I wish you hadn't quit the team," Derek said.

Hearing that was music to my ears, but I had to play it cool. "Me too, man," I said.

"So are you in?" Ruben asked.

I had to admit, I was tempted to bail on Valerie. I figured I could go to the library after batting practice. Then she walked up in a peach skirt and flip-flops. She had her hair back and her toes were painted bright red. "Ready?" she said to me.

Derek nudged Ruben. "Dude, I don't think Morelli's coming with us."

"We're going to the library to study," Valerie explained to Ruben and Derek. "You guys can come if you want."

"They have a baseball thing," I said. "Right?"

Ruben nodded. "Uh, yeah," he said, looking at me and Valerie. "We have a baseball thing."

"Okay," Valerie said breezily. "Have fun."

Oh yeah, I thought as we walked away in front of everyone. *This was much better than batting practice.*

Valerie and I spent almost two hours at the library. By the time we left, I had almost thirty flash cards on everything from treaties and battles to rivers and even a battleship. I knew when I saw those multiple-choice questions on the test I'd have no trouble picking the right answers.

"Don't make too many flash cards," Valerie said when we were outside. "You won't have time to study them all."

"Don't worry about it," I said. "I have plenty of time. I have a whole . . ."

"Two weeks," we said at the same time.

Neither of said anything for a moment. "So," Valerie asked at last. "Do you want to study again tomorrow?"

"I have practice. But I could do Thursday."

"Thursday it is," she said with a smile, before waving goodbye.

The next day at practice, Coach Darby stood at home plate with a basket of baseballs by his feet. McKlusky,

Shane, and Fish were playing the bases and Luther was behind the plate. The rest of us stood in line behind Wyatt at short. We were in the middle of a fielding drill I had suggested to Coach.

"Man on first, nobody out!" Coach called, giving Wyatt an imaginary situation. He whipped a sidearm ground ball that bounced toward Wyatt.

Now it was up to Wyatt to field the ball and figure out where to throw it. From a standing position, Wyatt reached down with his glove. Too late, though, and the ball rolled between his legs.

"Get down low, Wyatt," Coach told him. "Bend your knees. Keep your body in front of it." He held up another ball. "Try again."

This time, Wyatt moved quickly toward the ball, crouched, and made the play cleanly. He rose, squared his feet toward second base, and threw to Shane to get the invisible runner. Then he went to the back of the line, with dirt on his knees and a smile on his face.

Julian was next. "Runners on first and third," Coach shouted. "One out."

Keeping his hands in front of his body, Julian scooped up the two-hopper Coach had thrown. He popped to his feet, looked over at McKlusky, then shifted his focus to Luther. With a quick release, Julian fired a throw to home plate. The ball was off target, pulling Luther to the right. If there had been a runner, he would have scored easily.

"What happened there?" Coach asked us.

"E-6!" Shane shouted, meaning an error on the shortstop.

I was surprised Shane even knew what E-6 was! Maybe there was more to these guys than I'd thought.

Coach stood on home plate. "What should he have done?"

Nobody answered, so I said, "The easy out was at first base. Never throw home if there are other runners on the bases."

I saw Julian turn and glare at me. "What a surprise," he said. "Coach Morelli can't keep his mouth shut for one practice."

"I wasn't finished," I said. "Never throw home when there are runners on the bases *unless* the game is on the line. If the winning run was headed to the plate, then you made the right throw."

"Maybe it was," said Julian, obviously warming up to the idea.

"That's what I figured. So, nice play." I stuck out my fist.

"Got that right," Julian said, knocking his fist against mine. Then he turned to Coach. "Can I get another one?" he asked, like he had something to prove. This time, he flipped the ball to Shane, who swept second with his foot, then threw down to first base.

"That's two!" McKlusky shouted after catching the ball.

"How do you know the runner's out?" Luther asked. "We can't even see him."

"Then how do you know he's safe?" McKlusky shot back. He got into position for the next play. "I *thought* so."

"Is it me?" Caleb asked over my shoulder. "Or is the team getting a little attitude?"

"Hard to say," I told him. "McKlusky is talking trash to a runner who doesn't exist. I'll believe it when it's for real."

When we had gone through the line a few times, Coach led us through more drills. Next, we worked on base-running strategy. Then, tagging sliding runners. Finally, Coach called us to the plate, told us to get in line again, and said, "Let's work on bunting."

I was first. "Roy," Coach said. "Why don't you show us how to hold the bat?"

"No problem, Coach," I said, although it had been a long time since I had bunted. I got into my normal stance—the bat high over my shoulder and my feet even with the front edge of the plate.

"Go ahead and square up," he told me, gesturing for me to hold the bat out over the plate.

"If I do that, the other team knows I'm bunting," I said, not wanting to make Coach look silly for not knowing that.

"If it's a good bunt," he replied, "it won't matter."

Hearing some snickering behind me, I decided to

do it Coach's way. I held the bat out over the plate, bent my knees, and waited for the pitch.

But Coach had more to say. "Take a step toward the plate, Roy."

I moved up in the batter's box, then gripped the bat and stood in again. By then I just wanted to get my turn over with. I was pretty sure I wouldn't be bunting in a game anytime soon. Not the way I was hitting this season. "Ready," I told Coach when I was in position.

Coach pointed to my hands. "Careful not to wrap your hand around the bat," he said. "You don't want your fingers in the way of a fastball."

This was getting embarrassing. What next? Was Coach going to stand behind me and hold the bat *with* me? Had he forgotten who he was dealing with here?

Finally, Coach tossed an easy pitch my way. Holding the bat at an angle, I raised it to meet the ball, which was coming in chest-high. But instead of dropping to the dirt and rolling down the line, the ball popped up.

"Use your knees and body to adjust the bat," Coach told me. "Not your hands." Then he held up a ball. "Let's try it again."

I gritted my teeth and squared up again. All season I had wanted Coach to start coaching. I just never thought he would spend so much time on me. Thankfully, I laid down a beauty on the next pitch. With my head down, I moved to the end of the line, passing a lot of smirking faces on the way.

The sun was beating against the windows of Mr. Downer's classroom on Thursday. I was in the front row, scribbling in my notebook while Kenny read out loud. During a pause, Mr. Downer opened his eyes wide enough to see my pencil flying across the paper. "Mr. Morelli," he said, after telling Kenny to stop reading. "What are you doing?"

"Uh, taking notes?"

The whole class laughed.

"Hush," Mr. Downer told the class. He gave me the come-forward wave. "Let me see," he said.

While the people around me whispered and giggled, I walked to Mr. Downer's desk and showed him my notebook. "See?" I said.

Mr. Downer glanced at the notebook. He turned a few pages forward and backward. He stared back at me with those old gray eyes. "How long have you been doing this?" he asked.

"Since last week," I said. "Writing it down gets it into my head. I can't really explain it. But I know it works." I pictured the way the facts about Dred Scott had popped into my head when Camille was quizzing me at the cemetery.

"You don't have to explain," he said. "Just keep doing it. Any way it gets in your head is fine with me."

* * *

Valerie and I went to the library again that afternoon and Saturday, after my game. We had lost, 7–1, to a team we couldn't have beaten with seven of me. We took our table in the corner and cracked our history books. We read one chapter at a time, silently, then quizzed each other about what we'd read before moving on. I got to the end of one chapter, then turned the page.

"Oooh, Bleeding Kansas," I said, writing the term down on a flash card.

"It was a fight over slavery," said Valerie. "Not a horror movie. Sorry to disappoint you."

"Well, *makeup* test doesn't mean what *you* think it does."

"I never said it did."

Ignoring Valerie, I pretended to flip open a pocket mirror and pat my nose. "Did I pass my makeup test, Mr. Downer?" I asked, girling up my voice.

"I sound nothing like that." Valerie stared at me, like she had those times in class when I sank a bagball in her purse. But this time, her icy expression cracked into a tiny smile. "Can we get back to work? We've got twelve days until the final, and I'm not going to blow it because of you."

Actually it was eleven days, but who was counting?

· 25 ·

I wasn't sure which was more stressful, knowing that my history final was in a week, or that my baseball team had only two chances left to win a game. At least with history, I could practice every day.

When Mom came home on Wednesday night, I was at the kitchen table, reading a chapter from *The Call of the Wild* and making notes in the margins. We had a quiz the next day in language arts, and I figured that was a good way to get ready. Sara was sitting across from me, flipping through a magazine and glancing at her phone every few seconds.

"Why are you writing in that book?" she asked.

"Don't worry," I said. "I didn't check this out of the library or anything. It's my copy."

Mom put a large bag full of books and papers on the

counter. "I see," she said, taking a seat at the table. "I talked to your principal today."

I froze on the words *mortal fear,* reading them over and over again while I waited for Mom to explain.

"Do I need to leave the room?" Sara asked.

Mom shook her head. "You can stay, sweetie."

"So, um, what did he want?" I asked when I couldn't stand it any longer.

Mom pulled the book down so she could look me in the eye. "He said . . . that all your teachers have told him how much better you're doing in school. He said they're all very pleased with your progress."

"Mr. Groton said *that*?" I asked. "Are you sure he didn't have me confused with someone else?"

"I'm sure," said Mom, squeezing my hand. "I'm sure because I've seen the difference myself. You've been working very hard and your father and I are very proud."

"Thanks," I said, on the verge of blushing, but not wanting to show it. "That's, um, really great news."

Mom pushed herself away from the table. "Well, don't let me interrupt you. There's a lot left to do and I don't want you to ease up. But I know you can do it, Roy."

The funny thing was, I was starting to think I could do it too. Maybe getting a B+ on the final wasn't impossible. I'd know for sure after next Wednesday, when I took the test, especially since it was multiple choice and the answers would be right there in front of me.

· 26 ·

Saturday was our second-to-last game of the season, our second-to-last chance to win one. It was also the first hot day of the year. The sun started cooking as soon as it rose. No high morning clouds that burned off slowly. Just real summertime heat.

After breakfast, Dad drove me to Boardman Park to get in some batting practice before the game. He had on a T-shirt, cargo shorts, and a new Pilchuck High School hat.

"Nice hat," I said as we walked onto an open field. "Are you getting the letterman jacket to go with it?"

"Very funny," he said. "It was a gift."

"From the same person who bought you the history book?"

"That's right," he replied, stretching his arm behind his back.

"Well, at least you know what to do with this one."

Dad shook out his arms. He took the cap off his head, then he tossed it to me. "Take it," he said. "It'll look better on you."

"I hope so," I said, tossing the hat I had been wearing to the side and slipping on the new one. I gave the bill a bend, took two practice swings, then waited for the first pitch.

The next half hour was nothing but sweat, trash talk, and the ping of the ball leaving the bat. When the bag was empty, we decided to quit. "No sense wearing you out before the game," Dad said. Then he ran back to his truck for water and I sat on a bench in the shade of the grandstand, thinking this was the best mood I had been in since baseball season began.

Even the sight of Moochie Goodman slithering down the path wasn't enough to bring me down.

"What's going on, Mooch?" I said.

"What are you so happy about?" he asked.

"Do I need a reason?"

"Well, let me think," Moochie said. "You play in the rec league. Your team is winless. And next year, you're going to be riding pine in the dugout. So, yeah, I'd say you need a reason to be happy."

"How about you come down with cholera?" I said. "That would be a reason."

"Who's Cholera?" Moochie asked. "Some ugly girl at your school?"

"It's a disease, numskull. It killed thousands of pioneers on the Oregon Trail."

"I don't know what you're talking about," said Moochie. "But I do know that Coach Harden is coming to the park today."

That *was* a reason to be happy. But was Moochie just messing with my mind? "Who told you?" I asked.

"I overheard him say it to another coach," said Moochie. "So it looks like you're getting a second chance. Don't screw it up. Again." Then he walked away, laughing at his own dumb joke.

As the game began, I forced myself not to look into the stands. I hoped Coach Harden was up there, but I didn't want anyone else to see me checking. So while we were in the field, I kept my eyes on the ball. In the first inning, Shane knocked a slow roller down the right side of the infield. The second baseman was in position. But the pitcher stuck his glove out and deflected the ball toward first base, where it died in the dirt. Julian scored standing up and Shane was safe.

"That's one!" Luther said, pumping his fist.

Wyatt followed with a blooper that fell just in front of the center fielder and just behind the shortstop.

Caleb and McKlusky jumped up. "Go! Go! Go!"

A wild pitch put the runners on second and third with nobody out. Then Luther singled when his ground ball caught the outside edge of third base and skipped into left field.

"That's two!" said McKlusky as Shane crossed the plate.

"This is our day," Kenny added.

It sure seemed like he was right.

Hoppers bounced into our gloves. Double-play balls appeared just when we needed them. Pitches that could have been balls were strikes. As the game wore on, Fish, Kenny, and I weren't sitting next to each other on the bench. We were on our feet with our faces pressed up against the dugout fence, waving our arms like crazy every time someone else was rounding third for home. In the top of the seventh, we were up by three and three outs from winning our first game. *This* was my idea of fun.

"Do your thing, Morelli!" Caleb shouted.

"Have one," Coach Darby yelled.

The first pitch was low and inside. I hopped to avoid taking it on the toe. The second pitch was high and tight. I leaned away. *Okay, two and oh, now.* I knew the pitcher wouldn't want to go to three balls, so I figured I could look for something to hit. In my first two at bats, I'd walked and popped out. *Someone ring the bell.* I was hungry for a good pitch.

The next pitch was right over the plate. I turned on it, belting the ball—right at the shortstop! I halted in the base path, then went back to the dugout.

"Three outs," said Luther as we took the field for the bottom of the seventh. "That's all we need."

"We got 'em," Julian replied.

Luther looked over at me. "You know what, man?" he said. "You were right. This feels pretty good."

I wanted to tell Luther there was a difference between a lead and a win. That the last three outs were the toughest. But I couldn't bring myself to say anything that would make him doubt now. So I gave him a fist bump. "Let's win one," I said.

"Let's win one," he repeated.

I jogged out to play shortstop. To my left, Shane was in position at second base. To my right, Fish was digging in at third base. I walked over to him. "Three outs," I said. "You ready?"

"Ready," he said, his eyes focused on the batter.

That was when I took one last look at the crowd. And this time, I saw him. Coach Harden. I wondered what he was thinking. Was he impressed because the team he had come to watch was winning? Or *not* because the player he had come to watch was oh-for-three at the plate?

My mind raced. *Stop it. There's no time to think. Just play. Forget he's there.* But it was too late. Once I knew he was there, what came over me wasn't nerves. It was a deep-down need to put on a show.

The leadoff batter slugged a ball at Shane. But the ball stuck in his glove. By the time Shane got it in his hand, the batter was safe.

The next batter went to a full count.

"Nice and easy, Caleb," Coach called.

Caleb leaned back, raised his right leg, then launched a fastball by the knees of the batter. All around the infield, my teammates let out quick cheers. We'd gotten the first out. That was *huge*. I waited for the umpire to shake his fist for the strike-three call.

But he held out his arms. "Ball four," he said. "Take your base."

Now there were two men on and no outs.

Caleb stepped off the mound, muttering under his breath. *That's it*, I thought. *Take a deep breath. Then finish this.*

I rocked on my feet, ready for anything, as Caleb fired. The batter hacked at the ball, sending a grounder that rolled right in between McKlusky and Shane.

Another single!

Suddenly, the tying run was on base and nobody was out. Nobody on my team was smiling.

"Let's get it done," I said, banging my hand against the outside of my glove.

Then, a gift. A ground ball to my left. I could see how it ended before it happened. Field the ball, fake the toss, tag the runner coming from second base, then throw out the runner chugging for first. I would be the hero. And right in front of Coach Harden!

The ball bounced toward me. I ate it up. The runner from second base was on his way. I double-pumped.

But the runner didn't bite. He saw the ball was still in my hand.

"Three!" yelled Fish.

"Third base, Roy," Coach shouted.

No. Too easy. It's Roytime. Out of the corner of my eye, I spotted the lead runner sprinting home. With a perfect throw, I could get him. Throw him out at home. How impressive would *that* be? I pivoted to my right, brought my arm back, and sent a rocket to Luther.

But the throw was low. It went between Luther's legs and rolled all the way to the backstop. He ripped off his mask and sped after it. It was too late, though. Two runs were in.

"Everybody's safe!" the umpire hollered.

Now the other team was jumping up and down. They had runners on second and third with no outs. And the winning run was in scoring position. All because of me.

That was only the beginning of the nightmare. It didn't end until two more runs were in, our lead was gone, and we had lost. And it was all my fault.

After the game, I was slouched on the end of the dugout bench, replaying the throw in my mind. It was my first error of the season. *Why, why, why* did it have to come at a time like that? From where I was sitting, I could see Coach Harden talking to Dad and Camille. Dad nodded, then made his way down the bleachers, leaving Camille and Coach Harden alone.

As I sat there, my teammates passed by me. Most of them were speechless. I saw their heads hanging low. "I'm sorry about that play. That was my bad."

Fish clutched his glove tightly. "My *bad*?" he said. "Of course it's your bad."

"He's right," Kenny said, "you promised us you would play for the team, and not for Coach Harden."

"I was playing for the team," I said. "I was trying to throw the runner out at home."

"Don't even try to lie," said Shane. "We know who he was here for today."

"You should have thrown to third," said McKlusky. "That was the safe play."

"You said it yourself," Wyatt added. "Never throw home unless you're sure."

"Okay," I said. "I blew it. I was trying to be a hero. I should have gone to third for the easy out. Is that what you wanted to hear?"

"It's not about what we wanted to hear," Julian shot back. "It's about you keeping your end of the deal."

"We did our part. But you let us down." Luther shook his head. "I think I liked it better when we didn't care."

The guys were still grumbling when Coach Darby walked up to us. I didn't think there was anything he could say to fix the mess I'd made today. Especially not if he stuck to his usual garbage. But Coach Darby didn't tell us we were winners because we had played our best. Or that if we were gracious losers, we would really be winners. Or that we'd get 'em next time.

What he did was speak in a steady voice that filled the dugout. "I know this was a tough loss. But remember this feeling, fellas. Because when you do win—and you will win—I can tell you from experience it's days like this that are going to make it feel like you're on top of the world."

Or in my case, the bottom of the ocean.

That night, Sara sat on the couch at Dad's and asked me questions from the practice test in my history book. I could think of a million other things to do on a Saturday night, but there were only a few days left before the test, and studying *did* take my mind off baseball.

Sometimes the answer would pop into my head—other times I'd have to think about it. Like the one Sara asked me about the Westward Migration. "Which overland migration route passed through Nebraska, Wyoming, Idaho, and Nevada?"

"Easy," I said from the brown recliner. "The California Trail."

Sara peered at the book. "This is wrong," she said. "It should be the Oregon Trail."

"Shows what you know," I said. "The Oregon Trail didn't pass through Nevada. The California Trail did.

If you don't believe me, check the map in chapter nineteen."

Sara turned to the map. "Oh, right," she said, like she'd known all along. "It *is* the California Trail. The book is correct."

"I'm sure the people who wrote it will be relieved," I said. "Maybe you could help out with *all* their books."

Sara chucked a pencil at my head. "Since you're so smart now, maybe you don't even need me."

Dodging the pencil, I said, "You think I'm smart?"

Sara looked down at the book. "I was being sarcastic," she said slowly.

"No, you weren't," I said, enjoying the moment. "You think I'm smart. Admit it."

"Fine. I admit it. When you use your little brain, you show some signs of being intelligent. Are you happy now?"

Actually, I *was* happy. That was a big compliment from Sara. And it made me feel good to hear it.

· 27 ·

On Monday afternoon, Mr. Downer wrote a reminder in large capital letters across the chalkboard: FINAL TEST ON WEDNESDAY. Near the end of class, he let us ask questions about the test.

Wyatt raised his hand. "How long will it take?"

"You'll have the whole hour," said Mr. Downer.

Kenny had a question too. "Will it cover anything that isn't in the textbook?"

Mr. Downer shook his head. "The test only covers the book."

"How many questions will there be?" McKlusky asked.

"You will need to answer five short-answer questions and one essay question," Mr. Downer replied. "You can choose from three."

Wait—what? That had to be a mistake. My hand shot up. "Uh, Mr. Downer?"

"Yes, Roy."

"Did you say we had to write an essay?"

"That's correct," he said.

"So it's not multiple choice?"

A few people laughed. I turned red, partly from embarrassment, but mostly from panic. I was rattled like a batter who'd just been plunked.

"I explained at the beginning of the semester that the final exam would test your knowledge of what we had learned with an essay question."

Fear had overcome my ability to think straight. I was still a wreck that afternoon at the library.

"Don't worry about it," Valerie said while we sat in the study room waiting for Camille. "We're ready for this test, Roy. It doesn't matter whether the questions are multiple choice or essay."

Camille arrived a moment later. She must have seen the fear on my face because before she even put down her bag, she said, "You look like you've seen a ghost, Roy. You didn't go back to the cemetery, did you?"

"Roy thought the test was multiple choice," Valerie explained.

"That wouldn't be much of a final," said Camille.

"I'm glad you both think this is so funny," I said.

"I think it's the best thing that could have happened to you," said Camille.

"What? How?"

"What have I been telling you all along?" Camille asked. "Don't think about history as a list of things to memorize."

"So?"

"That's all a multiple-choice test is," she said. "A test of what you remember. But an essay will test what you know. What you understand. And how well you can communicate it."

"That sounds like a lot."

"In the cemetery, you told me the story of Dred Scott like it *was* a story. Like it was something that had happened to you. The details came naturally. An essay works the same way. Except you have to write it down."

"I don't know . . . ," I said.

"Roy, listen to me," Camille said, placing her hand on my arm. "You *know* this stuff. So let go of whatever problems you've had with this class in the past. You *can* be good at this, but only if you want to."

For a second, I felt like I was back in the dugout, listening to Coach Darby tell the team how good it would feel to win. I knew *he* was right when he told the guys they had to want it. So what reason did I have *not* to believe Camille now?

· 28 ·

I was sitting at my desk in my room, flipping through a stack of eighty-four flash cards at ten o'clock the next night, when there was a knock on the door.

"Can I come in?" Mom asked.

"Sure," I said. "I guess I can take a break."

Mom looked at the flash cards. "I came to tell you to stop studying," she said.

"You want me to *stop* studying?" I asked, not sure I'd heard her right.

"Give your brain a breather," Mom said. "You want it to be rested for tomorrow."

It reminded me of something Coach Harden had said about my brain. How it was a muscle, like my arms or legs, and I needed to use it well.

"Maybe you're right," I said, pushing the stack of flash cards away.

"I know I'm right," Mom replied. She tousled my hair. "What you need is a good night's sleep." She went to the door. "Now I need to finish *my* homework."

I rolled my chair across the room as Mom started to leave. "Do you really like college?" I asked her.

"Not always," she said. "And you won't always like school. But I know how good it feels when hard work pays off on a paper or a test, and I think you're going to know the same feeling soon."

"I hope so," I said, glancing back at the flash cards and wondering if I knew enough to pull off a miracle.

The test was three pages long. There were five short-answer questions and a choice of three essay questions. I had come to the end of section one, but the seconds were ticking off the clock. Carefully, I glanced to my right. Valerie had already written more than a paragraph of her essay! Maybe if the pencil didn't keep slipping out of my sweaty palms, I'd be further along too.

With a deep breath, I looked at the three questions. I knew I only had to answer one, but it still felt like the biggest do-or-die moment of my life. I just hoped I would have something to say about *one* of them.

I read the first question to myself.

Describe the differences between the Federalists and Anti-Federalists. What did they agree on? What did they disagree on?

> Be sure to discuss the national bank, protective tariffs, states' rights, and the Bill of Rights.

Whoa! I thought, on the verge of hyperventilating. I knew I had seen those things before, and I'd even made flash cards for most of them, but they were all running together in my head. I couldn't keep them straight.

I read the second question.

> Compare and contrast the United States before and after the War of 1812. Be sure to discuss how the war changed the country's relationship with Great Britain.

Yikes. That question wasn't any easier. I knew the British had burned down the White House, but nothing else was coming to me. I definitely didn't remember enough to write a whole essay.

I read the third question. By now, my heart was beating against my rib cage. If I couldn't handle this one, I was done.

> In 1858, Abraham Lincoln proclaimed that "A house divided against itself cannot stand." What do you think Lincoln meant by this? Citing evidence from your textbook, explain whether you agree or disagree with this statement.

I closed my eyes tightly. Everything went black. From all sides, I could hear pencils flying across paper. There was a cough in the back of the room. A lawn mower hummed past the closed window. Then, just when I was about to panic, words rolled across the blackness. *A house divided against itself cannot stand.* I had never heard that quote before, but I knew who Lincoln was. I knew he ticked off a lot of people because he was trying to do what he thought was right. And I knew what Camille would tell me to do. Put myself in his shoes—or his big black hat—and think like him. The more I thought about the quote, the easier that became. I imagined the quote was about my life, but instead of writing about my family or my baseball team, I wrote about Lincoln. There was no memorization. The facts just flowed from my head to my hand. *The Compromise of 1850, Dred Scott, Bleeding Kansas, secession, the Civil War.* I didn't even stop to think. I just wrote. And not a second after I put the period on my last sentence, I heard Mr. Downer say, "Time's up. Pencils down."

I dropped my pencil like it was a bat and I had just belted one out of the park. It was a good thing too, because I was going to need a home run on the test to pass Mr. Downer's class.

If only practice had gone as well that afternoon. During warm-ups, I went over to talk to Fish and

Kenny, who were playing catch by the fence on the first baseline. Four days had passed since my big error, and I thought maybe they had forgiven me. I stood a few feet away, waiting for an invitation to throw with them. I knew they could see me, but neither one said anything.

After a while, I'd had enough of the silent treatment. "Look, I said I was sorry. I was trying to impress Coach Harden. I blew it. What do I have to do to show you that I'm playing for the team?"

"Prove it," said Fish, without taking his eyes off the ball.

"What do you mean, prove it?" I asked. "I just told you . . ."

Kenny turned to face me. "That's the problem, Roy. You keep saying one thing but doing something else. If you want anyone to believe that you really care about this team, you're gonna have to prove it."

I walked away from my friends not knowing what else to do. Suddenly, the history test seemed like a walk in the park compared to baseball.

· 29 ·

At the end of class on Thursday, Mr. Downer told us he would be passing back our tests the next day. After the bell, Valerie came up to my locker. "Are you nervous?" she asked.

"About the test?" I said. "Not really. Well, maybe a little bit. . . . Actually, yeah."

"Me too," she confessed. Then she brightened up. "But, hey, whatever happens, we should either celebrate or do whatever the opposite is."

"That would be really cool," I said. "Maybe we could hang out this summer too, if you're not going anywhere."

Valerie smiled. "I'll be around. Just call me whenever."

I stood in front of Valerie like a statue, already trying

to decide how many days into summer I should wait before calling her.

Suddenly, she reached into her bag and handed me a white envelope. "I almost forgot. This is for you. Most people are getting theirs in homeroom tomorrow, but you can have yours now."

I opened the envelope and pulled out the rectangular card inside. It was an invitation to the graduation party. I knew everyone in the eighth grade was invited, but I doubted everyone was getting an invitation personally delivered by Valerie Hopkins.

"Why me?" I asked.

Valerie shrugged. "What are friends for?" she replied, before walking away.

Friends. I could live with that.

I threw my bag over my shoulder and pushed my way into the crowded hallway. Halfway down the hall, I couldn't resist. I turned around. The moment I did, Valerie spun on her heels like a top and vanished around the corner. She did her best to hide her face, but I was pretty sure I saw a smile.

On Friday afternoon, I swaggered through the front door like General Sherman leading the Union Army through the South.

Mom and Sara were sitting at the table when I marched across the room, holding the test Mr. Downer had passed back in class.

"Ladies and . . . ladies," I announced. "My name is Roy Morelli and *this* is the B-plus I got on my history test." I stuck the three pieces of paper on the refrigerator with a magnet and grinned. "Are there any questions?"

Mom jumped up and marched across the room. She peered closely at the test, like she was checking to see if I had used a marker to turn a D into a B. Then she turned back to me. "I'm so proud of you!" she said. She looked at Sara. "Do you see what your brother did?"

Sara wandered over to the refrigerator and examined the test as closely as Mom had. "Is this for real?" she asked me. "It *looks* real."

"Of course it's real," Mom told her. She put her arm around me. "It feels good, doesn't it? Finding out you could do something you didn't think you could do."

"I would have gotten an A-minus," I said. "But I spelled Lincoln with one *L* a couple times, so Mr. Downer took away points."

"I don't care if you spelled Lincoln with a seven. We're going to celebrate tonight," Mom said, and started to sniffle. "Excuse me, I think I need a tissue." Then she hurried out of the kitchen.

Sara was still reading over the test, shaking her head. "This is your handwriting," she said. "I can't believe it. This means you passed the class, doesn't it?"

I nodded. "Mr. Downer said my grade on the final plus my class participation was enough."

Sara was quiet for a moment. Then, slowly, she pointed her finger at me and smiled. "You owe me one."

"What do I owe you?" I asked, admiring the way my test looked on the refrigerator.

"I helped you study for the test. Without me, you never would have gotten a B-plus. You might not even be graduating—" She cut herself off as her eyes opened wide. "Oh my god, I just realized something."

"That you're a dork?"

Sara shook her head. "You're going to be in ninth grade next year. We're going to be in the same *school*." She walked out of the kitchen, mumbling something about her life being over.

"Hey!" I called. "It's no picnic for me either."

Part of me was dreading being the younger brother of a brainiac, but at least I was going to high school. All I had to do now was help my team win a game and, maybe someday, find a way to impress Coach Harden.

· 30 ·

I kept to myself before the game on Saturday. More than anything, I wanted my teammates to see that I was playing for them. But I also knew Fish was right. There had been enough talk. It was time for me to prove it. I only wished I could figure out how.

The umpire had just arrived when Coach Darby came into the dugout and told us it was almost game time. I could see into the bleachers. Mom and Sara were sitting in the front row. I spotted Dad by himself a few rows up. *Weird,* I thought as we took the field. Dad had said Camille was coming too.

"Let's win one," said Coach Darby, laying his hand in the middle of the circle.

"Let's win *this* one," said Caleb.

Quickly, there was a stack of hands and arms as we

got ready for the pregame cheer. I could feel my hand mixed in with everyone else's, but after we broke the circle, nobody gave me a high five or a slug on the shoulder.

I didn't think I could stand seven innings like this, so as I got ready to lead off the bottom of the first, I said to anyone who was listening, "If it makes you all feel any better, Coach Harden isn't even here."

"Look again, All-Star," said Julian.

Julian was pointing to the third row of the bleachers. Sitting next to Dad now was Camille—and Coach Harden!

By then, there wasn't any time to think about it. The pitcher had already lifted his right leg. He brought his left arm forward and snapped his wrist, sending a white ball of fury that twisted across the plate.

I didn't even get the bat off my shoulders.

"Strike one!" the umpire yelled.

Okay, I thought, stepping in for the next pitch. *That guy throws hard.* Well, the harder the pitch, the bigger the hit. Everyone knew that.

The 0–1 pitch burst out of the pitcher's hand faster than the one before it. He'd blown another one by me!

The umpire shook his fist. *"Strike two!"*

I moved away from the plate to get a look at the pitcher. He was tall, with arms that seemed to reach to the ground when he bent at the waist.

He was off to a good start, I said to myself. But let's

see what happens when I swing. I'd seen two pitches now. That was enough. So as soon as my eye picked up the ball on the next pitch, I put all my weight behind a swing that would have made history . . . if I hadn't swung a second too early.

Lefty had changed speeds!

"*Strike three!*" the umpire called as the Rockies cheered.

Dazed, I made my way back to the dugout.

"Here we go again," I heard Julian say to Shane.

"Just relax, Roy," said Coach Darby. "And remember, there's no shame in choking up."

Choking up? Was he kidding? If anything, the bat was too light. After three outs, I ran out to the field, already looking forward to taking Lefty deep as soon as I got up again.

My next chance came in the fourth inning. By then, we were down a run. I came to the plate with Julian on first base and one out.

"Nice and easy, Roy," said Coach. "We need base runners. Just hit it down and hard."

Oh, I was going to hit it hard all right. But not low. No way.

"Roy?" Coach asked. "Did you hear me? Think about the situation. We need base runners right now. Try to work the count and just get the ball in play."

I heard Coach. But I also heard the voice in my

head that was telling me to swing my best because this was my last chance to make Coach Harden remember Roy Morelli. And there was no better way to do that than by showing Lefty and everyone else watching who the big man in the game was.

"One fastball, please," I said under my breath as Lefty went into his windup.

And Lefty delivered. His fastball swerved through the strike zone and landed in the catcher's mitt with a pop. Then I swung through another one and fell behind, 0–2.

I felt my face tighten. This guy was really starting to tick me off. With every pitch, I was more determined to settle the score. I blocked out everything else—Coach, my teammates, the crowd—and concentrated on the next pitch.

It came more slowly than the others. I waited for it. I had the bat so far behind my back it was over my left shoulder. By the time I hit the ball, it would be so full of power there would be nothing left but twine, canvas, and a two-run lead for us. When the ball was close, I unleashed the bat with full force and waited for the sweet *ping* of the ball being hit. But the only sounds I heard were *whoosh* and *"Strike three!"*

Down again! This was unbelievable. He had struck me out twice! I tossed my helmet to the ground. It skidded in the dirt, then came to a rest at Fish's feet.

"You just can't help yourself, can you?" he asked. "It's like a sickness or something. You can't think about anyone besides yourself on the field."

"What are you talking about? I'm trying to get a hit," I said. "I'm trying to help us win."

"Keep telling yourself that, Roy. At least you can't say the rest of us are making you look bad," he said, walking to the plate with a quick laugh. "You're doing that all by yourself."

I looked to Kenny, hoping he would tell me Fish was wrong, but he was concentrating on the game. I grabbed a seat on the dugout bench, realizing I was running out of chances to come through for the team.

It all came down to the bottom of the seventh inning. No thanks to me, we were still within one run. But Lefty was still on the mound.

Julian led off with a single into right field. He barely even swung; he just put the bat on the ball and let the ball find a hole.

"Good work, Julian!" Coach shouted. Then he waved for the rest of us to stand up. "Come on, Pirates, last licks here. Let's make some noise."

"Come on, Wyatt!" Shane yelled. "Wait for your pitch."

I watched from the on-deck circle as Wyatt made himself small, shrinking the strike zone to the size of a dinner plate. Lefty would have to pitch perfectly, and that was tough to do with the game on the line.

"Good eye!" Luther cheered as Wyatt took ball one.

"Wait for yours!" Caleb called.

It was 2–0 now.

I could hear our section of the crowd getting into it. But I didn't want to look. I didn't want to know if Coach Harden was still there.

Wyatt fouled off a pitch, then ducked away from another one, making it 3–1.

"Let's go, Wyatt!" someone yelled from the bleachers.

The catcher had just returned the ball to the mound when Fish walked up to me. "Hey," he said. "You know you don't have to win the game by yourself, right?"

"I know," I said, making sure not to sound defensive.

"What I'm saying is, you might want to lay one down."

"You want me to bunt?" I asked.

A tiny smile appeared at the corners of Fish's mouth.

"You'll move the runner up—and stay out of the double play."

"That's good advice," I replied, knowing we both remembered how I had said the same thing to Fish earlier in the season.

Lefty uncorked a pitch that moved left to right across the strike zone, crossing the plate just below Wyatt's knees. We all waited breathlessly for the umpire to yell strike two. But he didn't. Instead, he held out his arms and said, "Ball four. Take your base."

And that was how I went to the plate with a chance to do it all. To get the best of Lefty. To win the game for the team. To impress Coach Harden. But all I could think about was something Coach Darby had said to me once. That sometimes a scout learned more by watching the other players than he did by watching the prospect.

But I also remembered what Dad had said about playing my best. So when I checked the infield and saw the third baseman standing back, I decided to do something I had never done in a baseball game.

After using the bat to knock the dirt from my cleats, I stepped deep into the batter's box, bent my knees, and squared the bat.

And with the game in the balance, and a fastball on the way, I bunted away my last chance to put on a show for Coach Harden.

The ball rolled slowly up the left side of the infield. The third baseman charged it, fielded it, and threw down to first to get me out, giving Julian and Wyatt time to advance. Now we had runners on second and third with one out.

I jogged back from first base, not expecting much from the rest of the Pirates. But there they were, lined up at the entrance of the dugout, ready to pound me on the helmet like I'd just hit a three-run homer.

"Nice one, Morelli," said Caleb.

"Way to lay it down," Shane told me.

"That's what I'm talkin' about," McKlusky added.

Then I passed Fish as he went to the plate. He stuck out his bat to stop me. "You proved it," he said.

"Thanks," I said, knowing it was the best out I would ever make. "I always got your back, Fish." Then I broke into a smile. "Your *way* back."

"Don't make me laugh now," said Fish. Fish pointed his bat at the plate. "I have a game to win," he said.

Kenny high-fived me when I passed him in the dugout. Then he turned his attention to Fish. "Come on, you can do it!"

And he did! With a short swing, Fish chopped the first pitch into right field. Julian took off so fast I thought he'd get whiplash. Wyatt sped around third as the right fielder came up with the ball.

"Go, Wyatt, go!" Coach hollered, waving him home as the throw came in from the outfield and the rest of us jumped up and down on the sideline. It was going to be close!

The catcher was on his knees, guarding the plate like it was made of gold, but Wyatt was charging like a mad bull. His feet were spinning like wheels, kicking up pebbles and dirt as he thundered down the base path. The throw came in high. The catcher reached up for it, snaring the ball, but leaving just enough space between his cleats for Wyatt to slide one leg through.

By the time the tag was made, Wyatt's hip was resting on home plate.

The umpire stood over him and spread his arms wide. "Safe!" he called.

We mobbed Wyatt at home plate. Anyone watching from the stands would have thought we had just won a championship and not our first game of the season. But that's the thing about winning: The harder the trip is to get there, the better it feels when you do.

After the celebration, when the dog pile had broken up and we had shaken hands with the other team, Mom was there to hug me. "I'm very proud of you," she said.

Sara was right behind her. "That was a great bunt, Roy. I'm glad you guys finally won."

Dad found me next. He was shaking his head and grinning. "I never, *ever* thought I would see you bunt in the last inning of a close game. But you did, and it was the right thing to do."

I gave Dad a playful punch in the gut. "I learned from the best, old-timer."

A minute later, Camille walked over with Coach Harden. Right away, Dad pulled her aside, leaving me alone with the coach.

"Congratulations, Roy," he said. "That was a heck of a ball game."

If Dred Scott had walked up and asked me for my autograph, I would have been less stunned than I was at that moment. I couldn't believe Coach Harden had given me another chance. "Thanks, Coach," I said, hearing the quivering in my own voice.

"If you're wondering why I'm here," he said, "you'll have to thank my friend Camille."

"She's hardly seen me play," I said. "What did she tell you?"

"She told me you had a good head on your shoulders. And after what I saw you do just now, I have to agree."

"The bunt?"

"That was smart baseball, Roy. And you laid it down perfectly. Had you practiced it?"

"Actually, yeah," I said, thinking of how Coach Darby had pushed me to do it right. "I had."

"Well, I'm impressed." He adjusted his hat. "Now, am I going to see you at tryouts next spring? Because you have all six tools, and that's what I'm looking for."

I stood up straight and stuck out my hand. "I'll be there, Coach."

He shook my hand just as I was swept up in a mob of my teammates. "We're going for pizza!" McKlusky shouted. "You gotta come with us!"

I joined the pack of Pirates swarming off the field, some of them still bouncing off each other and others tossing their hats in the air. Then, in the middle of all the madness, Kenny and Fish appeared on either side of me, slapping my back and laughing the way they did when we all got kicked out of the holiday pageant in fourth grade.

As the happiest one-and-seven team in the history of baseball rolled into town for pizza, I knew one thing for sure. When it had really mattered, when it was all on the line, I had definitely stepped up to the plate.

Acknowledgments

My gratitude to Jodi for bringing out the best in Roy, to Vikki for hitting another home run on the cover, and to Colleen for teaching me the difference between a glove and a mitt.

About the Author

Thatcher Heldring was born near New York City and has lived in New Jersey, South Dakota, Montana, and Washington State. When he was growing up, sports were a big part of his life, and he was pretty good at some of them. He's never played on a baseball All-Star team, but he has read a biography of every president from George Washington to Millard Fillmore. He lives in Seattle with his wife, Staci, and son, Jack.